A Tendency to Be Gone

A
Tendency
to Be
Gone

stories

Pamela Ryder

DZANC BOOKS

1334 Woodbourne Street
Westland, MI 48186
www.dzancbooks.org

Published 2011 by Dzanc Books
Cover art by Pamela Ryder
Book layout by Steven Seighman

"Three Men," "Sirens, Siren," "Tendrils, As It Were," and "Hovenweep" appeared in *The Quarterly*; "Apogee" in *Black Warrior Review*; "Solstice" in *Prairie Schooner*; "Arroyo" in *Frontiers*; "A Tendency to Be Gone" in *Shenandoah*; "Which Are Cinders" in *Yemassee*; "Overland" in *Conjunctions*; "Ark" in *Failbetter*; "Aquifer" in *Terra Nova*; "A Comfort in the Stones" in *The Texas Review*.

06 07 08 09 10 11 5 4 3 2 1
First edition September 2011
ISBN-13: 978-1936873036

Printed in the United States of America

CONTENTS

For Gordon Lish

And this our life, exempt from public haunt,
Finds tongues in trees, books in running brooks,
Sermons in stone, and good in everything.

—William Shakespeare
As You Like It

Snail, snail, glister me forward.
Bird, soft-sigh me home.

—Theodore Roethke

Hovenweep

We are too much in the open here: sky, sky, slick rock, heat, and high above us the circling birds. We are left too much unshadowed by the shape of them, escaping past the canyon walls, winging down the stone, unshaded by the deer-stripped juniper that juts above the river. We are unsheltered here these days we walk the rim. We take a trail all thorn, stick and mule deer spoor, a pebble-slide scramble of no place to step. These days I hardly find a footing—neither of us can—and when we are not watching the dark wing-drift on thermals or teeter over something dead, we are being careful. We are being slow and bent, clutching tufts unrooted by our hands, or stems of little-leaf toe-holding out here where the trail sends us scattering rock-broke dust and chips into the one of us behind. I get behind. I get looking into empty trunks of pinyon and lightning-struck logs for what is hiding from the rock-hot heat of day or what lies curled against the nights when stars are hardened and we are made closer by the cold. We search for what might keep us warm, spill our bundles made for traveling light.

"Poor planning," he says to what I pack for this Western weather. For this dry spell of wind-spinning needles and cracked-bark pine where birds sit bearded and squawking us past what they wait for on the hard-packed trail.

"Survival," he says when we stand on the ridge that once was river-bottom, and he shows me fossils of what was fittest. He points across the deep cuts of canyonland to what is limestone and Mesozoic.

"Layers," he says, when I bring out sleeveless for the sun and everything too bare and pretty for the nights we watch a far-off storm. We pull back the curtain, count lightning strikes: ledges, crags, blue-rock lit. Everything is too much in the open here is what we say across our bed. And back-to-back we wrap ourselves in whatever we can find.

Come mornings this trail is crack-treed, charred, not meant for walking on. This trail is meant for soaring over, for seeing down on when a wing-tilt shadow crosses us. This trail is meant for something skinkish, scaled or coiled, a belly-hot slither or split-hoofed step that breaks the rock and starts it moving miles down to the river. For the tough-footed clatter we hear just ahead of us and not this slow-go single file way of it when we make our way and one of us is always talking to the other's back. We decide along this up-and-down tangle of cliff rose and tamarisk: bend back a limb and wait or just let loose and hope who's bringing up the rear can keep his distance. We keep our distance. We keep a sentence short and to the point: I tell him he is always out of earshot; he says I can never be just one step ahead. So I try running, pushing through the brush, pretending it is just me out here, unheedful of the crumbly stone and ledge, me slim-hoofed sure past the scent of him, past his pant and breath, so far ahead that what I am hearing is just the wind that brings us bleak nights and early winter: the howl of it rounding the canyon, the hush of it in storm-struck pine.

These days we wait for storms. We wait for the sweet smell of ionized air, the charged drops never reaching us but freezing on a far mesa where it is too late to take cover, to find the rock that opens black and smoldered by old fires: a strike of flint, a strip of hide, the water-trickled wall and smoke hole where overhead the nights are starry-cold, tear-streaked, fallen. Nights we watch for meteors that light the silver plait of river and wonder if this dry-out spell of fall is early winter. But here it is not winter. Here it is the heat of blown-back storms and seamless sky. We say we will be long gone from here when winter comes—cleared out, packed up when there is talk of ice-opened stone, the river slowed, deer foraging the prickly pear. We see them mornings we are up before the heat: their long mouths pulling at gone-brown grass and seep-willow. We see them sundowns on the ridge, and moon-lit: the muzzled mist of their breathing, the white-tailed turn of them at a change of wind when they are spooked by the smell of us or whatever brought one down beside the trail: ripped flank, up-stuck legs, hooves. "They are so hard," I say, "and more like stone than something once alive."

"Basalt," he says, "Apache's tears," and "travertine," and names hard things. But sandstone is what this canyon is—wind-scoured, river-cut and carved, leached through and leaving behind the buttes and mesas, the solid buttresses that fall to pieces in a breeze. I tell him this wind, this wind, this dust all in my eyes. He says it is all just rock and weathering. He says we are just a wink in geologic time.

I peer into rocky pocked-out places I think are shelters, under overhangs to slip into unseen, flatten down and wait out a cold spell or an unslaked summer. He backtracks, finds me poking into river-rutted hollows. I show him where the stone is cold, where the hum of water runs against my fingertips. This must be where they hid, I tell him. This must be where they took water from seeped-down snow, left behind the char of their fires, stone jars, antler charms.

He leans two-handed on the ledge. He spits and sees the rock take it up: "Sedimentary," he says, "too high for water."

He says that nothing here was meant to live on alkali.

Some things were never meant to live at all, I think when we walk wide around the deer that lies beside the trail. We stay upwind of the smell of it, the double-time decay of it that happens in this open sky and heat, where there is no cool floor of forest or dappling of leaf and light to make it seem not quite so dead. It lies withered by what crawls along its innards, by this heat that tightens the sinews, shrivels the heart.

I want some twist of hair or clean bone to bring back for my remembering our walking on the rim. But there is nothing left of it he says I ought to touch: all buzz and reek where it sprawls split-legged, white-rimmed rump, hock, tail—the softer parts picked out by the birds. We see them walking on their wings, pulling at sockets. We see them unfurled on the rib-stretched skin emptied by whatever sort of vermin takes it from the inside out. Whatever sort of bug there is that scuttles under—but under is where neither of us say we want to look. I look for mortal wounds or signs of a struggle and wonder what might have killed it off. "Straggler," he tells me. "The weakest ones get left behind."

"Wait up," I am saying when he takes his long strides away from me, his step hard from climbing these hills.

"Slow down," I am saying when he climbs the mounds of me and I feel the huff and pant of him against me, the push and brace of him inside my up-stuck legs and flank he says is thin enough to feel the bone.

I feel the bone. I feel it through the smooth, stiff hair when I am on my knees and pulling the hide up from the hard-pressed earth or pressed and waiting for the rivered rush of him and the rock of me to take it up. I feel the water in the stone. I know the fissures in the face of the canyon where I kneel down, see into the dark, smell wet sand, damp wind. There are cracks in the rock that open onto darkened rooms with trickle-slick walls, etched with deer, safe from storms and open spaces. There are caverns colder than I am. There are unsheltered places in the noon-high dead of day where the rock is drier than our arid mouths upon each other, warmer than our bodies wait to be. He says he never feels the chill of my fingers, the drag of nails down the bare back of him, the unscratched hide of him he says is too tough to leave a mark. "Some things you never feel," he says. "Some things you just survive. But you," he says, "one winter here would finish you."

And we finish, find our clothes—mine are useless, lace-trimmed, tame; his are sturdy, woolly. We look past each other to the window, dress beneath a rib of moon. Each night the night is colder, with early dark and frost burnt off midmorning. Each night the heat of rotting deer smokes from its slit of tail and hindquarter, the dried-out mouth, the torn, picked-open parts. He finds the hollows of me. He tells me there is no place I am warm. He says, "Thinned-skinned," when I tell him fire is what we need, something flaming in the hearth against these cold-snap nights. We crack windfall branches across our knees, break sticks of pine, bone-brittle limbs. We make a bed of needles, tuck in cones, criss-cross tinder teepee-style. We stack the kindling that we hope will catch a spark. He makes his hands a cavern for the match-strike. He blows on ashes in the grate.

He says, "Weathering," when wind spins the dust of canyon rock through window chinks and wide-plank boards and into open spaces we keep between us.

He says, "Erosion," when we hear the rocks from upturned roots of juniper turn loose and rumble to the river. We hear the clack of antlers. We hear hoof-clicks on the stone. The wind taps twigs to the window and we pull the curtain back to see the distances of stars are just a finger-breadth apart. We touch, flinch. Stars streak down. They make no mark against the black or burn above the tree line, survive as starry pellets that pit the slick rock, make this trail of pebbles we slide on.

I take this trail down switchbacks, deer paths, past the skin-down hide, new slides of stone split by last night's freeze and morning thaw. I cut through water birch and cactus paddle-tail with shriveled hearts of prickly pear still hung on. I climb bare-armed, heat-spent; push through fireweed and creosote. I hunch down where sandstone makes a roof and dim room; I duck in from the heat. There is a sound of dropping water. There is the chill of water moving in the dark. I sit cross-legged, smear my scratches with the silty bottom of a seep.

I hear him call—it must be me he's calling—"Come on out or you'll just be lost." But I stay listening, waiting for the far-off sound of him: words muffled by sheets of stone when I am tucked chin-to-knee between the sheets of our cold bed, talk told to folded pillows, to the slow pace of river that widens the bedrock between us, follows the fault line we are on.

I lie flat to this rock floor, crawl to the shank of light and lookout. It is all sky, wind, downspin of birds. It is all overhang and scarp, hoodoo, spire, the twist and course of river that does not show how deep it cuts until it's done. Until we are in the open here, without our separate shelters—the spaces that we make with no space for the other.

"Hermit shale," he says when he finds me, when I show him the scorched stone of their fires. Where they fed flames, drew herds of deer on walls that wavered in the heat. But these are cold rooms now, long-gone cold before the two of us were bending here, believing something must be hidden in the sand.

We sort through shards: find nothing left unbroken.

We sift through cinders: find chips of bone; no amulet, no charm.

"It was all too long ago," I tell him.

"It was in another age," he says. He pulls up rock chunks that line the fire pit. "Feldspar," he says. "Paleozoic."

"Over," I tell him. "Gone," I say, when we see the smudge of a palm against the wall, a tracing of a hand before they left without a trace.

"Higher ground," he says, and how they overhunted, followed game, found rocks that trickled sweeter water.

"Metamorphic," he says, and shows me milestones, watermarks—the path away a hardened ripple of river mud. He shows me cracked stumps, heartwood, rings that mark years of gone-dry river with nothing left to drink or douse a fire. The years of only winter, drifting, packed-deep snow.

"Packed up," I tell him when we lay our bundles on the bed that holds our things for leaving. I cull my too-thin clothes and leave behind the twigged and ragged pieces, whatever is ruined or all wrong for weather here and home. We sort and set aside. We find grains of sand, grit, soot.

"Just one last look," we say and take our one last time to walk the rim. But time is what want to I take—I never had his way of walking. I lag behind until he is a far-off step ahead of me. Until he is the crunch of rock, a snapped-back branch, a distant thunder-crack. I watch the bunch and sweep of clouds above the farthest mesa, the curtain-fall of early-falling snow. It is weather never reaching us, wind-whipped away from us to let us wait for what is coming, or what is worse.

Birds waver on updrafts, drift broad-winged down. They drop to the pinyons, flap unsettled, clawed, clack-beaked at me where I am pulling at the flat-out hide. Where I find it emptied inside out by what winds inside the skin of it, lives inside of what is dead, what is sun-sheltered, safe, kept from freezing nights and open air. Where it is thatched into the gone-brown grass, stuck deep to this last stubble of the season where I am bent and finger-digging, unclinging earth from the edge of it. Where I free it from, find no grub, no worm. Where there is just this sun-cured skin beneath the hair, slick rock smooth and clean enough to wrap around me, warm enough to shrug a winter off in, high-tail it out downriver in and gone. Where there is just soft-sprouted grass beneath the skin, pushing up pebbles that once were stars, pale grown around a rock-hard clot, the heart of it that shriveled to a stone.

The birds sit hackled where I pass under, where I turn off this trail through scorch-grass and scrub. I make my way through sparkweed and nettle, unscratched by thorn and sticker in this new skin. I crack through brush and break oak, ash. I clutch knots of roots that sink deep in the ridge.

I press my belly to the wall in narrow places, my face tight to the rock face; my mouth and lips give up water to the stone. I climb through layers, ages, epochs—rough-fingered in the bluff, wedge-footed in the shift and slip of where I thought was solid. I crumble rock, break stars. Pieces glitter where I step. They scatter, slide away, falling from this star-high ledge that lets me see the way down to the river. It bends through gorge and chasm. It turns past cliff and cliff. It winds past this windy place I stand out on and pull the hide around me. The place I pitch away this cold rock of a heart.

I send it spinning headlong, smoking dust where it clips the outcropped rock, and rebounds wide, unbroken.

It drives an arc through open space: wingspread, spread-winged. Down the stone.

Tendrils, As It Were

We are on our way anywhere in our house and they are in our way: flowers, on the backdoor stairs where the shards are swept; on the front-stoop step where the fence is picketed; on the upstairs stairway, awaiting the tuck and boxed dust of an attic trunk or the space on a table in the cut glass we are undecided who sent. I am undecided and sidestepping. I am holding off and holding the flowers I held: stem-wired five-and-dime flowers, bunched by an unraveling of grosgrain, spilling down the stairs, lifting at the close of our windy door.

"Clutter," my husband says. He is the one who does the deciding, the one not waiting for the wind to change, the one not caught midstream or on the fence. I am snipping the zig and zag of one loose thread with scissors, the coming-undone of the streamer of it in my hands. My hands are not hands you would like to have.

Hard, you might say, if you saw my hands—homely, big-knuckled hard and unpretty enough for flowers. Flowers for sleight-of-hand hiding the clumsy jut of my hands as they come cowering from a cuff, as they stick wild-stalk sprouting up a sleeve.

They are wrinkled and ravaged, and bird's-foot crooked. They are vein, crease, scar. They are weathered and blighted—the worse for wear—from digging gloveless in the garden. What was once the garden is a stone's throw out of season by the backdoor stairs. If you would find me there you would find me unstrangling the banister and freeing the pickets. You would find me pulling up what grows before flowers of the catalogued and cultivated kind. The hardy and the hardly invited: stonecrop, silverweed, and cinquefoil, finding a fingerhold in whatever might be subterranean and unspaded: things rusted, glinty, rotted, root-bound. But not the roots of plants I planted.

Not the mail-order kind that need a certain soil and time for looking after. I turn pages, place unfilled orders, select and unselect, undecided.

"Just do all blues," my husband says and points to pictures: delphinium, periwinkle, foxglove.

"Perennials," he says, when I am gritty in the grain of me, in nail and whorl and packed in treads. He hangs a rag on the backdoor nail. He puts a mat on the backdoor step. He points.

"Rows," my husband says when he sees me muddied, kneeling. When he sees me making space for flowers. When he brings me string for keeping what might be coming up in line. When he puts a pillow where I should put my knees.

"A bird in the hand," he says when he sees how I have overwaited and what was pulled out is pushing up again. When he sees this is no bed of roses, this is no garden path.

"Did you ever decide?" he says. "Did you ever pick anything?"

I did not pick the ring on the finger where a ring should be. I did not pick the smooth-handed man who did the measuring of the end of me that is my ring finger.

"Bigger," he was saying, upsizing me across the counter, jangling his interlocking loop of rings, checking the nicks and chips in me: the too many mishaps marked in my hands. His hand, unveined and uneventful, held me down on a pillow meant for showing off stones. A string wound round my finger would have been enough of a measure.

"Enough for the knuckle," he was saying when he pushed the silver on and over the split tip and sticky bleed of me, the stub of nail. When he twisted what he had into the knot of me that makes a joint, the rough of me made rougher by a ring trick of silver and his smooth hands. My husband was pointing to the rows under the glass.

"Show us something simple, something," he said, "uncluttered."

But it is clutter that comes up in my garden: a scramble of scrappy weeds and wildflowers. More leaf and thorn than petal, and not enough petal for what I need for holding in my hands. Henbane, gorse, and lady's thumb is what I get and what I get for wanting to see what comes by unbidden: seeds dropped by birds in droppings or spun in on streamers, on fluff, on dust, conjured by the breeze. Tendrils curled into cracks and pushing beneath the pillow.

He does not want the garden pillow when he wants to put a pillow where I will put my hips. He does not want some store-bought rose. He does not want some tied-back vine. He wants the part of me that wants to watch what crawls away when I upend a stone, the me that leaves the turned-down bed, steps down the stairs, out to the darkness of the garden. To the tatters of string unmarking what was never planted.

There is a window above the garden. There is lamplight that shines on the glass.

There is a vine that leads along the fence and winds where a vine can hold a wall. There are tiny flowers in the creepers you can see in the dark if you are looking, if you know what you are looking for.

Have you looked at night in the lighted windows in the shops that sell flowers?

Have you seen the sameness of flowers in rows, on shelves, in cold, glass cases? Have you seen them stripped of leaves and trimmed to an evenness of stalk?

His flowers—he brings me flowers—bend in the cut glass on the table. His hand is clean and smooth on the coolness of the bed.

"Growing season," my husband says these cooler mornings, when he sees me chucking stones that keep surfacing. When he wants to know: what went with what seed-spilled and unstaked packet. When he says there is a solstice fast approaching and where am I? "Biennials," my husband says these first-frost mornings, when there are rose hips to pick in the brambles. When there are beggar's ticks stuck to my sleeve. When he sees my hands large, caked, mud-flaking. When he sees me briar-scratched, bleeding.

When he says blood from a stone. "Annuals," my husband says these breezy, all-blue mornings.

There is a ring on my finger big enough for my knuckle. There is a trick to getting it off. Have you seen the trick of rings and watched the shimmer and slide of silver? Have you kept your eye on whatever keeps moving? Have you watched the loop of rings and wondered where they come apart?

There are flowers on our stairs tied with what the wind would snap around me. Each stepping-over unpetals what I had to hide me, frays the ribbon meant to bind it. I pick up scissors. I cut away the pieces I am losing: a ribbon more unwinding every time I hold it in my hands.

Three Men

He is kicking down shingles. He is down to the tarpaper, showing us what the weather has done, where there is trouble. He has his ledger, his list of bad news, his pencil. He is estimating the damage of what went undone for unpaid years, figuring time-and-a-half for patching over before the rain will teach us a thing or two.

He is in the cellar sniffing dampness. "Must," he says. Sweating pipes, sump pump and septic where it should be cut and dry. He knows water tables. He knows weep holes. He knows what seeks its own level. He has his ear to the ground and his foot in the door. He has sheetrock, trip wire, nails. He has traps. He knows varmints. He knows claws and where to clap the clapboard. He is telling us to cross our fingers and knock wood. He is inspecting for specks and telltale tunnels. Crouching. He has his ear to the ground.

"Borers," he says, with his head in the crawl space, showing us where the sill is settling, where there will not be a wall.

"Partial to hardwood," he says, hammering a hollow sound where it should be solid. "It's just a matter of time," he says.

"Just a matter of give and take," says my father, who comes without calling. "Give them an inch and see what they take," he says. "I did. Look what happened."

"What did?" I ask him.

"Ask your mother," he says.

We have termites in the baseboard, carpenter ants in the attic. We have galls in our oaks, moths in our woolens, skeletons in our closets. "Click beetles," says the man. "June bugs," he says. He taps the freshly painted plywood where other owners tried to whitewash what was.

"Listen," he says, thumping the threshold. "Dry rot. Dry as a bone." Prefab and friable is our wall. He is sliding in a crowbar, crunching, crackling, splintering wood, and plying us with destruction. "Damage," he says.

He is looking at electrical, calculating kilowatts. We are ungrounded, inadequate, and underwired. We will blow fuses, start fires. We will outrun our meter. We will black out at the rate we are going. He is telling us to up the ante and the amperage.

He is dark in the cupboard, whistling, lighting corners. He is in the pantry, listening for scampering. He is nosing along shelves, blowing on a turd. "Rodents," he says. He is telling us hairless tails, saying gnawing is their nature. They will chew our wiring, short our circuitry, start a smoldering in the walls. "Vermin," he says. Rats in the rafters. We have mice, we have voles. We have options: poison, pay up, or pay the piper.

"Hell," my father says. "Use traps," he says. "Spring-loaded. Use bacon, use cheese. That'll teach him. That'll get him. Got me," my father says.

"What did?" I say.

"The way to a man's heart," my father says.

He is pacing off closet space, speculating. He knows conversions. He knows his boot size in metric. He has treads, skid-proof soles, safety toes, grommets. He has reinforced seams, flannels, double-duty pockets, loops. He has places for hinges, hangers, hooks, eyes. "Weevils," he says. "Worms." In jerseys we have them, in worsteds, in wovens: the clothes on our backs when our backs are turned. He is telling us cedar for safekeeping what we want to save or store or what we must give away.

We have crows hunched in our oaks, waiting for a handout. "Pests," says the man. "Pellet gun. Lead shot."

"Stuff and nonsense," my father says, unbuttoning his button-down. "Scarecrow," my father says, shirtless.

I am folding clothes to give away, deciding what I am too old to wear, what is too worn, what will be rags. I am making piles, separating keepers from maybes, courtship from marriage. I am being reasonable, putting things aside for sentimental reasons, deciding what can be taken in, let out, or left alone; deciding which to patch, which to mend, and whether to bother. I am making room for smaller rooms, clearing out and making space for every one of one man's chambray, silk, and chamois shirts in my closet. I am sorting and smoothing, laying seam on seam, laying the past to rest. I am dipping into pockets that have been through the wash, searching for a last-ditch dollar or dime, hoping against holes nothing has slipped through or slid by.

He is in the sink, the man, over the hole and snaking out the drain. He knows sewer smells. He knows augers. He is plumbing the sludge, telling us what we have in our pipes is not water, scaring us with lead. He is telling us there is no telling. He is unprying pipes, unstripping the wrapping. He is pointing out pinhole leaks and pressure surges. He is tearing the gauze and talking asbestos. He is digging his nail into what comes crumbling down upon us. We are not up to snuff, says the man I call. We are not up to code. We are not in compliance. We are not correctable. We are wrapped around his little finger.

"Harmless if you never breathe," he says.

"Masking tape," says my father.

He is looking for leaks, drips, water damage. He is popping loose bolts and frozen nuts, pulling down plasterboard. He is staving in the warp and rot of a waterlogged riser. He is telling us we do not want to know what is behind the stairs.

He is tearing out tacks, ripping up the wall-to-wall, slicing through the broadloom. "Carpet beetles," he says. Eggs in the nap, in the pile, in the shag. He is rolling up shreds of what was our rug, telling us the night to put it out and pile it up on the curb.

We are walking uphill in our house. We are lopsided and unlevel. He is tilting the vial and shifting the bubble. He is swinging on a beam, showing us sag, showing us what must be cut away, what will never hold.

My father is shaking his belt loops, showing me what still fits. He is telling me what I will not remember, reminding me of when he wore a cutaway, and what she wore—my mother—and where it is preserved safe from weevils but no longer white. He is telling me what was set aside and what was saved. He is telling me what will be mine if I want it, if I cut corners, squint past imperfections and promises, just make minor adjustments.

He is telling me he has a tux in camphor, how it is shrinking in storage. He is telling me about his first house—their first house— how everything seemed smaller when he came back for a last look. How he must have looked to other owners when he asked them for a look around. How he must have said: Yes this was my house; this was my daughter's room, this her mother's.

I am standing with him in what was once our yard, our stoop, our front step, looking into windows that I once looked out of. I am standing with my father beside the giveaways that went unsorted, the things we lost, set out and left behind when we left our house. I am standing by the bridal bush that bloomed beside the door that let us into the house that was our house.

I am walking with him through that house. Past the place I slept and waked and asked my mother what made the nighttime sounds I heard in our house: the planks that creaked in empty places, the pipes that clanged when no one ran water, the wind-whistle in the room without a window. I am lying in the bed where I asked my mother what made the hum and silence of a house that held us, stood for us in any weather.

I am hearing my mother not answer.

I am hearing her, and hearing him—my father—and their nighttime voices from separate rooms. I am listening hard, hard-pressed for answers past the plasterboard beyond the sheetrock, in the sheets and pillows. I am hearing a house crack bit by bit, lying awake in my bed, looking, seeing the first signs of giving way: a chip of paint or plaster on a pillow, the hairline in a wall. Seeing what was narrow grow with the closing of a door, the setting down of a dish.

"A little spit, a little spackle," my father says. "Elbow grease."

He is in our yard. He is soil-sifting and sampling. He is sifting a jar of our silt, stop-watching the settling. We have runoff. We have delayed drainage. We are sodden, gritless, ungraded.

He is toeing up the turf around our oak, kicking moss where we should have grass. He has mud in his treads. He is not afraid to get his hands dirty. "Grubs," he says, holding up a hunk of our lawn. We must hoe it under, till, hope.

"Nuts," my father says. "Spread a little lime."

He is out at the fence, swinging the gate off its hinges. He is rocking the pickets. "Post beetles," he says. He is telling us to pull up stakes and get out while the getting is good.

He is snipping our shrubbery, chopping our tree. He is chaining a stump, lumberjacking our timber, telling us to pull and hack. He is saying roots are our undoing: strangling pipes, splitting our foundation.

He is splitting our siding, shaking the cedar. He is showing us where he must gut and sledge. We are, he says, past repairs.

My father is out on the curb, picking through the throw-aways. He is what I have folded. He is holding a shirt to his shirtlessness. He is showing me what to save by taking a stitch in time.

He is on our roof, chin to a ledge. He is upside-down-eyeing the overhang. He is under the eaves, checking the downspouts for splash and seepage, for overflow and uphill water. He is looking for ice jams and leaf dams, following where a gutter is leading.

He is climbing from our roof. He is taking the path of least resistance, sliding down cellar doors, kicking in basement windows, feet-first cracking cobwebbed glass, going underground. He is snapping shards beneath his boots, scuffing in the muck. He is squashing what comes crawling under a foot and into a seam. He is finger-digging decay from our corners. "Night crawlers," he says, "pill millipedes." He is poking a nest of them under a stud. He is showing us what is left of our substructure. He is showing us struts that are sinking and becoming soil.

He is showing us where we should step down, kneel in the wet, wipe a hand along the wall. Saying we should see for ourselves how the damp will ruin the boards and where he stacks them sawhorse high, safe from warp and early rot. Showing us where he works into the night, planing the pine, smoothing the plank. Custom-sizing to our specifications: snug at the shoulder, tight to the lid. Uninsulated. Knotty and unvarnished. Sanded or stained. Silk-lined if we'd like.

He is saying not to worry, he will be right here—one level down from the after-dark answers, one flight below the rattle of the spare-room door. He will be down here—listening for our breathing between each nail he is driving. Waiting for an exhalation to become a rattle between each pull of the saw.

He is saying: it is here. It is all down here. It will be down here and waiting. It will be our final shelter.

Out of the weather, waiting to enfold us: the earth, the ground, the source.

Arroyo

We are past the point of no return, the two of us: I'm with the map and she's at the wheel when we sight them on this moon-bright stretch of sage, smoke tree, and stone.

We are past the point of pulling over, turning back, when we spot them where the trees thin out, rocking their coyote lope or singing in a head-up howl.

We are saying that they make their way by movements of the moon that motors over us through tree-spaced glimpses of the river, or else by circuits of the stars. That they follow traces of blood-littered leaves on the water sliding by us, hunting by the scent of something wounded, slipping stream-bottom stones, or by something they are sniffing on the wind.

But tonight there is no wind. Tonight is just a hush, hush, slap of limbs and leaves we pass, the breezy speed of rolled-down windows, the flap and whip my hair makes as it floats above the glass or winds itself back in around my mouth. Tonight is just a yip-yip-howl from somewhere in the foothills, the folded-over crinkling of the map. We hear the clink of coins up on the dashboard, the smack of bugs against the glass. We watch the road and what it is that flits into our light: sage moths and roadside skippers; hairstreak swallowtails, mesquite gnats. They leave us wings and sprays of powder. They leave us splintered legs, soft-bodied splatters red and wet. We stop to wipe and scrape the windshield, to talk of being almost there, to take a closer look at which way we are headed.

But I am way ahead of where we are. I am where the line of two-lane ends in black and then goes gray and dotty just beyond the fold. It is a raggedy edge where we are. It is a soft fraying of paper. It is a hairline that starts too small to mark and squiggles to the water that must be passing past us, the wall the tops of cottonwoods are making of our view. Here and there it opens: a space of treeless stream where once a fracture and flow of rock turned the river in its stone bed to cut a muddy strand.

We stop to crack our legs. We stand out where moonlight paves old river-bottom stones, stream-smooth shapes undersided grit and wet where once the water was. My fingers spade the pieces up: this one river-carved into a coin, this one a moon, this one a tear or a toad; and this one worn long-bodied: "A coyote—almost, don't you think?" I tell her. "With notches almost where the legs would go."

"Almost," she says when we are on our way, checking our clock, clocking the miles. When we see their moon-long shadows ride the arid flows of stone. We see them staying with us, headlong running until we lose them where crusts of rock twist the river and the road bends us around.

We wind back to the water. We say this must be the way. We say this must be the scenic route—the four-cornered split I am splicing. This must be what we were missing: the piece that goes just where the fold becomes a hole: an edge we might drive off of, a bridge I must have burned. A detour, a road out, the parting of the waters; the part we lose when she wants north, me south. When we miscalculate mileage, figure how much farther. When we wish that we were closer than we are.

We count inches. We compare the scale of miles. We say it seems we have been circling, and we lean the map into the light. She grips the wheel and says, "Where are we?" But I say where we are is somewhere off this map. We tug west from east. We tear along where we have overfolded. We crumple. We shred. We litter the road with ripped-up scraps that flutter in the mirror of our rearview. They drift and scatter torn-winged, taillight red. The dark comes in. The dust comes up. We rumble on.

We make time.

We have our clock. We have our compass, our sense of

direction: our watertight bubble on the dash. The arrow swings and wobbles as we swerve from rut and ditch, from what we just miss and slide into each other for: the jolt of a jackfoot rabbit, the scuttle of a spadefoot toad. We watch a poor-will wing over. It lifts and hurtles unstruck past the place our headlights let us see.

We have trouble seeing. We are bleak-eyed, sleep-struck. We stop. We squint up at the stars. We say we have never seen so many in this hemisphere, that we have never seen so far.

"The air out here," she says, and we sniff. We smell something near. We breathe what blooms at night—paper flower, paleface, white horse-nettle; paloverde, ocotillo and chaparral. We smell the tamarisk, tires, tar. We feel the heat of this hardpan air.

We see the heat-bent shapes of cottonwoods where smoke rises red and steady. Where flames set the river lit with sprays of poked-up sparks and something dark is turning split-legged on a spit. We watch the swing of lantern light, the flash of trees. There are shadows, there are voices; there is singing from a sheet-bright tent. We lean and try to listen: a hymn, familiar—and lose it where the river makes a mirror, where the still waters lead us and the river takes the road for a turn.

We take our turns. We waste no time. I had my turn another time there was a newer moon, a shift of stars, a man to make my wishes with. We had our wishless stars. We had our sleepless nights. We had our nights I took my turn at talking past the point of talking, past the point of wishing I would hear him call my name. Nights we were wishing the night would pass and we were just passing the night, passing each other in the hall, circling and stepping aside to let the other pass. Nights we were facing off, turning away our eyes, our tears. We took our turns at wishing, at watching out, at looking the other way.

She looks the other way. She says she knows when it is I nod off and hope she hasn't noticed. We watch the road. We share, we shirk. We read signs: no passing, no stopping, no services. We are closed for the season; we are closed for the year, for forever and for always. I would take him always. I once took him always. Until a do-us-part, a death. I have seen the coyotes. I have seen them scatter, circle, close in around a kill. I have seen them safe and singing in the hills. Safe from harm. To have and to hold.

I had him once to hold. I have a stone to hold. From this day forward. We go forward, we watch the road, we listen for the hills. I listen to the stone: there is no singing. Once there was singing; we were singing. We were kneeling and we sang the words we knew. There was a ringing bell, fingered rings, him never to be slipping through my fingers, my folded hands. There was a hymn, a hollow sound. There was a joyful noise. There was a moon-white paper marked with my name, his name. The paper was unfolded, unfrayed. We were not afraid. We would take a chance. We would last. We would stay awake, see signs.

We see signs: last gas, last water, last chance.

We see what we can stay awake for: sage-spread flats, wire fences, emptied towns. A head-down Appaloosa; the knee-tucked carcass of a cow. A boarded church, sprung-loose boards, a steeple. A fenced-off square of saltbush: headstones set in crooked, the color of the moon. We turn off. We shine the light. There are markers, mounds. There are pawed-up places in the hardpan, roots, rocks, bones turned up. There are seraphs in the stones— faces, tears, cracked wings. There are traces of dates, days, names buffed away by sand.

We come on names and crossroads. We read the way we think we ought to go. We talk landmarks, town lines, lodging. We say smooth sheets, clean beds, road bends. We lean into each other. We miss mileposts, points of interest, populations. We pass an outpost of progress: a one-horse town where we should ask for help. Where a map would tell us: please make local inquiries. I ask if she is tired, if we should trade places or push on. I say the names of where I think we are: "Cholla," I say to a crib, a trough, a cross on a shack. "And that—that must have been Bajada."

And Pero, Mañana, and Bad Water. And Wikiup, Blood Rock,

and Safe-From-Wrath. We watch the road and blink the far-spaced roofs of moon-glazed metal by. The smokeless chimneys, a wind-wheel stilled, a cottonwood corral. A cut of road that fades its way to timbered tunnels in the hills. A town where someone struck out for the hills, staked a claim, struck a seam. Where someone once mistook a glint, a strand, for silver hidden deeper in the stone.

I can hide the silver. I can twist away the hair that floats above the glass. I can catch the fraying fronds of me, lose them in my road-wind tangle, hide them in the deeper parts unsilvered. I can keep them from the mirror that the rolled-up window-light is making of the dark.

I can hide the mirror. I can look away and tint my mouth a shade it used to be. I can dust my face with powder, pretend away the lines, pretend it is my color where the paleness of my skin pulls tight along the bone. There are shadows I can hide.

There are shadows on the valleys, along the old arroyos, on the pebbles of the streams. There are shadows in the foothills where the coyotes go. Where they trot their head-up reckonings according to the moon. It is said they sing for the moon. It is said that their singing makes the moon to rise, that they play their tricks with the stars. It is said that the stars are theirs. That they keep them in their dens by day, deep and silvered in the rocks. That there are stars to see if we strike out for the hills, follow the scent, come quietly along, kneel down. There are coyote songs to hear in the rocks if we are listening, if we lift up our eyes. If we watch a poor-will passing, wings unfolding, calling itself its name in singing.

We think about singing. We think a song might wake us, but neither of us knows the words of one the other knows. We try to sing the hymn we have heard before: the rock, the cleft, the cleft-for-me, the water and the blood. But we are thin and weak of voice; we are poor of will.

We listen for the voices from the rills. We listen for the coyotes and the stone to sing. But there is nothing that we hear. There is nothing overhead but stars, nothing where the stars go dark on distant hills but dens of stone.

They take them to their dens. They take the jackfoot rabbit and the fold-winged bird in their tight snap of coyote jowl. They catch them head-down drinking waterside, unaware and scratching in the litter of the smoke tree leaves, or sleeping in a bramble. They come coyote skulking their soft-foot, ear-flat growl. They circle, signal each other, crouch low. They catch them by a feathered keel, a fur-hidden rib, a scruff-haired neck that hides the beat of blood. A snap-fast shake can break them. Coyotes break them, bring them quietly along—wounded, outwitted, outrun; bring them stunned and undone to their dens, held spent and limp in their long dog-mouths. Sometimes there is a struggle. Sometimes at the entrance of the den there is a desperate pawing at the dirt, a clinging to the pebbles that all roll down. Sometimes before the coyotes drag them splay-legged into the dark they see the final stars, the last moon. They breathe the smell of burrow dust, of old blood of brethren. They leave signs of the struggle: a hollow-boned wing unwoven in its folding for the tunnel; a twist of skin-cleft hair; a jackfoot torn; a downy ear; an eye uplifted last for hope, for help never coming.

Held stilled of breath and head-down to the stone.

I hold the river stone against my ear.

We hold our breaths to hear.

We hear the clock tick on the dash, the tick of metal of the motor cooling down. We hear the crack and break of something in the scrub. We shine our high beams. The stars go dim; the distance goes away. Bugs buzz in. Moths brush by our faces. They leave a trace of powder on their off-course orbits to our lights, mistaking them for moons.

We have made mistakes, we say.

We have made a mess of it.

We make our hands a cup for catching river water, for washing blood from the windshield, for catching coins of starlight from the faraway cold. We take the water from the hollows in the stones where the river makes a cup.

We are picking up stones: the flint-chipped shards of arrowheads, the chunks smoothed by the road of river, the river-worn shapes of tears. We are road-weary and worn to tears.

We put pebbles from the river into our mouths to keep the taste of water in our mouths when the water will be far. When we cannot make a cup.

I am dipping into the river, dipping up the silver glint of minnows in the cup I am making of my hands. They are slipping through the spaces of my fingers. I am drinking from the river. I am dipping up the water to my mouth, washing the taste of him away. I am on my knees, dripping water, head-down drinking watered moon, splashed stars, dashed hopes. My hair hangs in the water. She takes my hair all tangled in her hand. Takes me where my neck meets skull and she can feel the pulse of blood. She takes me under. Pushes me into the place she wants my mouth. She wants me drinking from the river. She wants me head-down in the water, mouth to stone and split-legged in the dark. She finds the pebble of me, the slippery banks of me where I am winged and unescaping. Where I am sliding stream-bottom stones, stirred on by the scent of something wounded. I am face down and willing. I am unfolding, unstruggling, undone.

We are drinking from the river.

We are where the moaty dust of desert streams into our lights. Where moths light bent-legged beside us, tent-winged and tamping at the sandy strands of river with the curling parts they have for mouths.

We are drinking from the river.

Where the seraphs of the river come too close for drinking, drift wing-down flailing in the final swales of stream. They spin near the spits of sand where we sit, where we drift and lean into each other, toss into each other, touching only in the places that are bends in the road. They struggle and circle wing-pinned to the surface, out of reach of each other or the slide-by of a leaf.

We try to take them from the water by their wings upfolded. We try to lift them two-fingered where they will not tear. But they are fragments. They are shreds of wings and powder. Minnows rise and gulp the dust. We watch their mouths and the break of bubbles. We hear the sound of the river on the stones.

We have heard that the sound of the river once was singing. It is said that a clamor of praise once rang from the rocks. That the cobbles of the river called out and the wind did speak.

That a stone in the hand will be silent; will not answer a voice of the stream. That the river-bottom stones sing still when a wing passes over, or where tears or the light of the stars makes a spangle on the water.

It is said that blood—not tears—will spring from the eyes of a spadefoot toad. That we lift up our eyes to the hills; we will see from whence cometh our help. We will keep watch on the stones of the hills with our eyes lifted up until there comes our time.

There will come a time. There will come a time that the watch will not keep and my eyes will keep coins of the stream-flat stones. My face will take the pale of the hardpan dust. I will take the color of the hills, the color of a leaf on a smoke-tree twig that is taken by the water, slides a slope of stones, bubbles up and comes turning where the river eddies on the mirror of the water—an arrow in the compass-spin of river.

It will lead me from beside the still water.

I will have a bed. I will make an unmade bed of stone. I will pretend a pillow for my head. I will pretend the pile of stones will keep me, will keep me. That it will keep me safe and where I am: face down to the rock, powdered with the ashes where the rock once was burning.

I will be a rut, a ditch, a talus of the slope, a strewn-away stone. I will be a mouth filled up of pebbles for the taste of water when I have no hands to make a cup.

I will be a pawed-up tangle of hair, a bone the color of the hardpan dust dug up.

It is said that the spadefoot toad can change its color, can make itself the color of the dust or the color of a sun-worn leaf or the color of the light of morning on a stone: first sun of morning on a stone.

We set our sights along the edge of hill that takes the earliest of sun. We look for the soonest light along firey rim of banded rock that heaved up when the earth was molten and unmade, when the river was a slow red lunge of blood-hot stone.

We watch for coyotes. We see them trot and stop and sit long-haunched, chin-pawed down. They tent their ears and turn their heads to hear.

It is said the coyotes hear the stone where the stone is still a river—deep in the earth where the ore is a ribbon of metal that flows. That they cock their heads to the sound of the flow of the rock, of the selfsame stone that spins the needle of magnetized north.

It is said that by this coyotes find their way, know the rock of their direction. That they speak to the stones, and their moon-high howl is the way that they talk, confuse their prey, offer up praise. That they run with a river of stars in their mouths, stay safe from wrath, restore their souls.

That they call to the hills—the coyotes—and circle.

They signal. They sing.

We watch them track along the clotted rock before the sun is up. They slip into the clouds of sage before the flats are burning. We see them lost into the spaces of the hills. We see them reeling in the stars. We see the last of stars along the river where the minnows hover up to drink the air.

We take our last drinks in the first light. We wait for light enough to see our faces on the surface. To see the counter-clocking fins that wing the minnows up. Their mouths make circles on us in the mirror. We watch the circles dip and flatten, ever-spreading are the wrinkles in the water that widen us away.

We watch the sky where it is past the point of morning. We watch the fading of our fix of stone-round moon. We stop and see the signs we have seen, but the boards are bent and broken, with worn-away words and arrows pointing directions unknown.

"Which way?" she says, and we watch the moon dissolve above the ridge where lids of clouds blink close the dawn-day stars. We see the two-lane turn to dirt and disappear.

We hear our words dwindle away.

"This is right," we say, not knowing.

"This," we say, "is where we want to be."

Where we tore our map, tore our wings, tore the stones from the bed of the river with our fingers. Where the river bears down in its bed and wears the stone to coyotes. Where it wears away the moon, makes tears of the rocks, sweeps the fingers of the branches bending.

We are where the river takes a curled-up leaf of smoke-tree in the current, curves the banks, touches our mouths. Where the river sends it turning. Where it points the petiole of it west and north, and east and south.

We are where the smoke-tree leaf is leaning on its curve of midrib, caught in the watercourse, withered and spinning.

Where it slides itself away with water pouring in to fill the empty cup.

In the Matter of the Prioress

In the matter of the prioress and her associations, most recently the source of much distraction and debate, herein is found a just account—and apologies for its inadequacies and omissions—as she, the prioress, is seen returning late to Arden Abbey, and astride the bishop's horse; it known to be the bishop's by many a husbandman, groom, and ploughman in these parts, owing to its proclivity to free itself from stall and halter, and set its lusty energies upon their unsuspecting mares, resulting in the number of roanish colts birthed each spring; its unencumbered outings due, in part, to aged brother Benedict, who, feeble of intellect and prone to fanciful imaginings since struck in the head by the hoof of the beast, remains *non compos mentis*, and thus is given simple chores about the abbey stable. (One may blame his rantings of diabolic impieties this past Epiphany upon either his infirmity of mind or upon the unfortunate switch in the scullery of medicinals for spice—mandrake root for ginger, jimsonweed for mace—which were stirred into the Christmas Eve ragout, resulting in excited agitation of the brothers and their midnight capers in the moat.) Too frail for bleeding, leech, or mortification of the flesh (other than infrequent penance with the hide of a hedgehog), the aged brother denies himself the fraternity of the refectorium (where he but gibbered in his gruel), takes no ale, but has his sup of scarburgh fish on a stool at the stable door. Moreover, he forsakes the comfort of the dorter to spend his nights bedded in a hay-trough, waking to find the bishop's steed untethered, unsaddled, and its unrestrained desires spent. Known, too, is the refusal that the bishop makes to have the creature gelded, despite his (the roan's) attacks upon such persons foolhardy enough to greet the bishop and his mount with a courteous sweep of the hat or a pat on his (the roan's) nose. Dare not turn one's back upon the beast, even with attempted truce of apple core or carrot! He seems to care for none except the bishop, and remains unrideable by most. Yet, upon that very roan has the prioress been spied, bare both of head and of foot (the order, as you know, goes not unshod), her chestnut hair unbound by veil, snood, or plait. Her seat, it should be noted, was not of the side-saddled style considered suitable to a gentlewoman (which she had been the years I knew her before she left secular life), and was not of a position appropriate to her present station, but—and all pardons to the following account— the good prioress was observed mounted in full straddle on the bishop's beast with her skirts askew to accommodate that seat and, with her garments in that most awry state, displayed his loins (the roan's) hale and withers sound. In this very manner the prioress has been seen astride the bishop's horse of evenings late, and not without the bishop.

And not without one Vinegar Tess—this the name the prioress gives the abbey cat; and if one would doubt its presence on such an outing, or would wonder how it sits upon a horse already bearing two: it crouches in the saddle sack, concealed except for the protrusion of its bushy tail from out the bottom. And there it rests, most comfortably, it seems, this creature that the prioress is hardly seen without, though it be as ill-tempered as the bishop's horse. Attempts to stroke the brute or offer a playful hand toward its kittle (which the nuns call "George") will result unjustly in a painful stripe upon the hand, even with a bribe of fish, or sniff of cattish nip, or soothing lilt of coddling voice! It seems to care for none beside the prioress and her holy women, and if one were uncertain of the goodness of their hearts or unfamiliar with the motto of their work—*Laborare est orare*—one might perceive they dote upon this feline pair in the manner that witches of a coven are said to do.

And in this way the trio is seen gadding about the lanes along the hop fields, and past the barley coming ripe. Past, too, the sisters bending with the poor to bind the sheaves and bring the harvest in—the order well known for their help throughout the season, and for the handsome gloves they sew of hide and give out to the reapers at a halfpenny each, for the weeding of the crop, and to shield them from the thistles. The prioress herself is most skilled in needlework. Long have I kept the counterpane she sewed to be our wedding bed—crewel-worked with silken threads and roses made from lover's knots—and kept, as well, the pair of doeskin riding gloves she made and fashioned to fit my hand alone. The bishop wears a pair himself, and well needed would they prove to be, as the reining of so headstrong a horse as his requires. In this task his hands remain well occupied; but her hands—those of the prioress—are clasped about the bishop approximately at the level of his belt. And she, the prioress, rests her chin upon his shoulder and her mouth does press close beside his ear, her lips nearly upon it—perhaps providing him instruction to a bridle path of shortest length for returning to the mother house—this according to the hermit who lived beneath the bridge at Kemp-on-Wold (and who, alas, was presumed perished when the Wicker spilled its banks this past wet spring). And further, the prioress does press herself upon the bishop's back in excess of what she must to prevent her unseating—despite the spirit of the stallion and the urges it so readily displays, the canter of the roan is of a gentle slope—and her landing in a haystack. The hapless miller boy (alas, dead now one week since caught by the cuff in the grindwheel gear) reported that near the noon the pair arrived at Penfield Pond and there they did refresh themselves after so warm and close a ride: the bishop first making himself shirtless; the prioress lifting high her habit in the shallows, sprinkling herself and spewing him with water from her mouth; the bishop catching her along her skirts, and both becoming wet—these behaviors, of course, owing to the midday heat. Perhaps fearing vapors from the dampish cloth and the coming of the cool evening air, they then placed their garments upon the hedge for drying out, whereupon they spread upon the saddle pad a wedge of cheese, cups of wine, the wastel-bread they carried in a cloth, and partook of it with keen appetite; and also of potherb the prioress fetched from the forest land for them to eat (skilled she is for knowing mushroom, leaf, and root in both cookery and nursing of the sick). For sweets, they carried no confectionery and found no fruit, but ate of honey that the prioress fetched from within a crab tree's knotty hollow—the comb full with bees—until she uttered some queer speech, making them fly off at her command, and without malicious buzz or sting. The fated boy then heard the sounds of their merrymaking from within the thicket where the millpond empties out—their murmurings and laughter, both—which he attributed to their fervent midday prayers and exclamations of Heavenly joy—but witnessed nothing more. By chance, a passing hunter, intent on taking stag and fowl from these lands of his lordship, told in his confession his notice of a man and maid he spotted in the glen, and that these two slept *puris naturalibis* but for the ferny blanket that they wore, and open to the air except in places that their secret parts did touch and limbs entwine— saying that he saw the maid possessed a mark most curious upon her breast, being horned much like the moon in crescent. (The hunter, of whom I speak, was found to hide within his poke a brace of partridge and the fresh-stripped pelts of a coney flock, and admitted setting snares throughout the wood; such evidence went hard against his case and he cannot, alas, be here to verify the tale—now a fortnight tried and hanged of poaching.)

Something is amiss, as well, inside the abbey: the chantry often empty at Matins, Lauds, and Prime, as reported by persons making pilgrimages and stopping there for shelter from the night. All classes of persons are to be found within these bands of wayfarers—stockfish mongers, cunning women, purse pinchers, and pardoners—who, lacking a sense of propriety, will peek shamelessly in any window or spy at any door. Unreliable as such reports may be, during hours when holy folk are best about their devotions, a novice was discovered within a monastery cell, kneeling by a monk who lay upon his pallet, his bedclothes undone (as reported by one who now is well upon his way to view the holy relics, and alas, remains *non est inventus*). The prioress denies all manner of diabolic rendezvous, and claims the novice sister knelt only in an attitude of prayer and thereby received her spiritual instruction. And she, the prioress, is known to spend her nights stoking the scullery stove, decocting all manner of degenerate plants, among them nightshade, spurge, and rue; and in her kettle there she stews them with eel and newt, and the flesh of nightjar, swan and smew for what she would say are batches of medicinals for the treatment of pestilential maladies and pox, and for the curing of contagion. Yet the simple and superstitious folk that seek her skill as apothecary are ignorant in the methods of modern science and astrology, and hold that these draughts are potions that loose earthly desires and summon up the craft and work of witches, and that she carries antidotes of bedevilment within the holy pyx. Poor Brother Benedict reports partaking of the Eucharist, and to his great dismay, discovering that the said elixirs, mixed with penitential blood let from the brothers, were dispersed instead of sacramental wine, and passed by the prioress so that all were made to drink. The unfortunate fellow suffers from aberration of reason, so this account, and all that he relates regarding the unwholesome acts by the brothers with the stabled mares, must be taken *cum grano salis*.

It is, then, most urgent that one not base judgment upon gibe and innuendo. *Ipso facto*, inquiry must be made in order to dispel rumors of necromancy, and unsully the repute of the holy house. Yet, upon confrontation of these reports of ungodly vice, the prioress heeds not gentle word nor admonition. By no appeal to her upon our years of friendship—no, not even by our brief betrothal before she took the veil—will she yield to offer explanation. Indeed, all that she will make as her response is her reverent smile and "tsk, tsk, tay" or a sweet "we thank thee for thy visit" while all the while she coyly twists a length of loosened hair upon her fingers—and is it by some new decree they now may wear their locks unshorn? Any continued investigation is hindered by the antics of the kittle, George, which, though first may seem to be a charming sprite, begins to skip and leap about making the mischief particular to young-born creatures, knocking Bible and breviary from off the shelf and proceeding, with upraised tail, to foul the missals strewn about, and to cavort at length until, at last exhausted, it stretches itself out. More curious, still, is the account of the aforementioned novice, who noted unsettling events during discourse with the prioress on her displeasure at the laxity of abbey life. This young woman, (alas, now silent since her holy vows) reported that she, the prioress, beckoned to the mother cat to come and sit upon her lap, and began, in some harsh foreign tongue, to whisper shrewdly into its flattened ear while its slitted eyes grew bright as coals in hell. Thereupon it arched itself up, doubling its size, and giving spit and hiss with most evil intent! From out its maw were raised what sounded to be the howls of roasting souls and their ungodly oaths, until it coughed and gasped to disgorge the creatures it had most recently eaten—mice, mostly—but, and in evidence of its being no ordinary mouser, birds as well, and beetles of a swarm, a small snake, shrew, and bat—all most rotten, chewed through and leaking of their blood; but some, having been swallowed whole, remained alive enough to pull themselves from out the slime and end their torments by creeping to the lighted hearth, where they burst with great noise, spark and soot, but for the bat which landed upon the prioress. Wet, and shriveled as a fig, it clawed along her wimple with folded wings to perch upon the holy rosary around her neck, and there it hung head down, as if it were a pet. The prioress seemed little disturbed by its familiarity—indeed, she stroked the thing and set upon it her kisses, and, untying the restraints of her bodice to bare a moon-shaped mark upon her breast, placed the creature upon herself to suck. No natural milk spouted forth for its nourishment, but blood, instead, adribble; and with much delight—as shown by its chirps and squeaks—the creature drank of her, while its tongue (much like a serpent's) wound between its thorny teeth. And when it had enough, she pulled it from her teat, cleaned it with her tongue, and breathed her breath into its mouth until it stretched full its leathery wings to fly out through the window.

Such episodes as this put to an end all attempts at further inquiry.

The bishop, too, is struck dumb in matters of the abbey, and on the subject of the prioress as well. Not knowing the holiness of his heart and devotion to the order, one might suppose he and the prioress to be confederate spirits, or that she keeps him silent by some unnatural device or spell. Question him as to the need for nun and priest to be shut up inside the confessionary at more length than appears adequate to recount sins and receive penance—and he says nothing. Ask what good he thinks can come of descending the pulpit, silencing the choir, and halting his sermon when the prioress arrives after the service has begun (her mewing Tess in tow and hindering all in their psalmody)—and he has no reply. Ask why the brothers end the mass in baying at the moon like hounds, or how the sacristy happens now to hold a damask vestment and altar-piece stitched by the nuns, not with the pattern of a dove, or holy cross, or angel, but instead with serpent, snail and crow!—and he is silent. Seek to reason why the coverlet that the prioress fashioned for our nuptial bed (all these years cedar-kept and folded tight against decay) should now bear vermin and wool-eating worm—and his tongue will not serve him to speak. And ask, then, why she, the prioress, should not be stripped of all her holy clothes, shorn and fully shaved to best expose the marks of enchantment which she may keep well hidden by her hair, and then searched within her secret parts for tokens of the Devil—and the bishop suffers the *lapsus memoriae* one expects in those decrepit of wit!

The truth will not be found within the fancies of one dotard of a brother so feeble-minded as to be a vexation to himself, nor the quaint superstitions of rustics, nor reports from peeping pilgrims who sidle past the abbey walls or skulk about the shrubbery. It will be made evident in an account by men of honesty and credit who seek to preserve the merit of the order and reaffirm its worth to the gentlefolk and tenants of this district, and who, by their reverence for the church, pay firstfruit and tithe as best they might. Having no interest in these matters other than in fulfilling the appointed duties of investigation, cleansing the order of slander, and ensuring the holy repute of the good prioress (for whom my admiration is unfailing), I humbly conclude the aforesaid account, with regrets for any deficiencies therein. *Satis verborum.*

Dominus vobiscum.

Apogee

Nights like this, his music comes before his coming. Nights like this, he cranks out jangles in a minor key, setting caged-up kitchen birds tinkling their bells, beaking the tight-wired cuttlebone while he plays louder than the turned-up salsa, sharper than the glass-chip chimes the storefront consejera keeps for spirits in her window on the street.

Nights like this, my Pepe gets himself hanging tailside up inside his hoop. He knows, I think, I have to look. He knows I have to watch him unfolding feather by feather, turning himself inside out, unfanning me his underwing—the parts of him his evening blue goes pale. I talk his clicky bird talk to him. I tell him what he likes to hear. I never say what he must think are flights of passing nightingales is piped up music. Blue notes and downbeats. Trills. Riffs. Reedy tweets and bells from a speaker where a list of flavors that says "Señor Mantecado" shows the hand-painted pictures of the push-up pops he brings me and the crushed ice in paper cones, the slick-winged bars and rock-hard confections in a cup. He clucks low, clicks soft, talks back. But what he has is nothing like a human tongue.

Some nights I let him bite me just to see inside his mouth—just to see that tough old ball he's got in there, the kind you see inside a whistle. I let him drag his hard-hooked beak along my lips. He breaks the skin. He draws a little blood. He won't let go until I smooth his ruffled feathers and a bit-off bit of me slides down his throat.

Some nights I have to drop a cover on his cage—a flowery square I stitched to keep him quiet: peonies from the scrap pile, primroses in chintz, a swatch of bleeding hearts cut on the bias or left over on a bolt. The tail end of something unpinked, unsnipped.

A piece of what I am all day pushing beneath a needle. What I am two-handed feeding the teeth that nip up from the dark and snatch away the cloth. I watch out for my fingers. I stay inside the space the shaded bulb keeps lit. I watch the folds unwrinkle over places where my blood has rusted up the metal plate. I see the needle strike and spark until I'm seeing stars. Whole nights I sit here bending to the light. Tacking down the miles of trim without a tangle. Watching frill uncoiling from a cone. From a spool. A spin of rickrack and ribbon. Of twill. Tassel. Fringe. Finishing a brim in pom-pom, a pocket or lapel in piping, the edge of *pantalones* in satin stripe or braid. A border of sequin. A helix of spangle. Pushing along inches of prints, plushes, crinkly knits. Watching yards of polished cottons full of flowers of the kind I never see in yards go by: marigolds for beds and borders, begonias and tea roses for an edge. I sit rocking the treadle. I sit waiting for the ring of chimes above my needle clicking, above the clamor from the downstairs *la cocina* where a stove steams late into the night.

Nights I hear the cooker boil and rattle above my buzzing down a seam. I hear the squawk of something on a block. The chop. The blood-spurt beat. I hear Señor Mantecado while he does a slow burn: snapping my scissors at my Pepe when he starts somersaulting in his hoop. When he starts his all-night fretting at the sight of us together on the foldaway: spilling his seed-cup, flinging sunflower and thistle, sowing the linoleum with fruit-treat mix and beak-cracked corn.

"*¿Qué pasa?*" Señor says when my Pepe plucks the bars off-key. He bats his plastic play-bird and shreds up his newsprint floor. He sits and sulks amid the piles he's made of perforated spirals. He peeks out at me from pulled-out feathers, seed-flecked shit.

"*Mi Amor,*" he says in a voice that's not quite mine.

"*Mi Corazon,*" Señor Mantecado calls back through the curtain in the doorway.

"*Mi Alma,*" I hear him answer from my back room bed while

my Pepe pulls himself along me, hauling himself up beak first then foot-over-foot in a little fist.

I feel his claws in places I am soft. I feel the scales he has for skin. I say, "*Mi Pepe parjarito*," and he nuzzles closer. He nips a little. He lifts his tail, squawks out a word I never knew he knew, squirts down his dirt.

"Who taught you that?" I ask him, but he doesn't need say. I can tell it's Señor Mantecado anytime he sends that tune a turn ahead of him, has me listening for those hollow bells above the whirring of my spools and bobbin, above the plugged-in cooker pop and sputter of *el pollo* in the dented pot. It sits sparking from a socket where the dark-haired combed and braided ladies pluck pins, hack feet, melt fat. Where they tear off cock-combed heads. They smack their basting spoons against the pot side, singe, sear, turn up the radio and sing. They sweep out feathers rising on the kitchen heat, up flights of bricks, through up-tailed shirts, past shades, sills, smokestacks on a flat-topped roof, to chicken-wired skylights of a high-rise slanted to a low-rise moon. To the ledge I sit along and listen for the tune that comes while he is still two turns away and curbwise leaning on a slow leak.

He drives down-clutched through puddles, splashing where the hydrant sprays the street. Standing where the metal is cut out, his bare-armed and undershirted bulk against the shelf. He serves up the packed-hard crystals in a paper cone—lime green, purple, blue and red—sunset colors slightly melted and looking inside lit. He stands just out of sight where it goes dark inside the rivets. He stays behind the beams hot-wired stars send down—strung out along the overhang just out of reach of someone reaching up for something cooling on the tongue: a Rockety Pop, an Astro Bar, a Cygnus on a stick. Something he brings to my bed on nights I am waiting: a Double Whammy Sickle, Galaxy Splits in assorted flavors that leave my sheets sticky; Crater Cones pressed into sprinkles; Dog Star Dips stashed in my freezer—crunch-coated or moondust dipped.

Sunspot Clusters in a cup, stored where the cold smoke hisses underneath the silver lid he lifts. Where someone steps right up to hear the thumb-clicked slide he makes inside the scoop. Leans a little over on the counter edge for the pitch of wind from polar regions, the whisper of a meteor passing too close by a planet or sizzling through the dark in dreams. The scoop descends into the rush of galaxies locked up. The skeins of stars I wish I had for stitching. The spaces light-years deep where El Señor keeps an asteroid under wraps. Where he has a comet turning on its tail, aurora borealis captured in a paper cone, a peel unspiraled one-piece from something citrus. The doubled-fisted dips he drizzles with the *el jugo de naranja y pina, el jugo de limón*—flavors that the night and heat will water down. Down sidewalks slanted wet and running, turning cobblestones to gemstones the colors of a neon buzz; past padlocked gates, reeled-down doors, awnings cranked up for pigeons roosting wing-tucked with one eye out. A clock-slowed Sunday night wound down, seen from the billow of windows, through the swell of orchids on the doorway curtains. From the turned around straddle of kitchen chairs we stick to, the stud-punched plastic backs hung with what the two of us were wearing. The two of us front to back in my backroom, my flowered bed—petals of the wrinkled roses spreading under us— while my Pepe picks his heart-shaped lock, slides down the rungs, and rides the caged fan tied with ribbons back and forth.

El Señor rides. I hold on.

I dig my fingers in the arrowed hearts along his arm, his inked-in skin, the blue-lined bird that pulls a banner he keeps empty, waiting for somebody else's name. For someone falling for his fly-by-night proposals in some other part of town. Another neighborhood he just breezes in and out of, is what I think some nights when whole days go by without the hollow bells that have me trying on somebody else's lace-trimmed trousseau, a tulle-draped headpiece, the made-by-hand *mantilla* for a bride. Gets my stitches in a pileup, threads pulled, seams puckered. Sends me down the walk-up stairs. Pulls me down the iron steps suspended doorway high above the sidewalk, saves me from the treadled beat. It frees me from the storefront *consejera* where I am held palm-up upon her table—readings, fortunes, futures, *se habla Español.* She has potions. Mojo wish-beans. Premonitions. Knows all, sees all. She knows jinxes. Hexes. Ouija. She has spells and genuine birthstones. A cabbage rose where her hair is coiled. Hoops in her ears. Cards on the table. Sticks of incense. An incubus kept bottled up. You can buy her press-on planets, a forty-watt moon with invisible wiring, a foldout sky of constellations. She unfolds my fingers. She follows my skin folds, my seams and stitches. She touches the scars my Pepe makes.

She says that I'm unlucky in love when she finds what passes for my lifeline. She says that the moons of my nail beds make predictions impossible. She says she is out of jinxes. She is short on spells. Low on potions. She is unsure if my gemstone is jasper, jade, or opal—perhaps it is turquoise, or maybe tourmaline. She says that the Ouija is sleeping. The wiring is faulty. The future is dim.

She tells me this calls for drastic measures. Methods more dependable than palms, smarter than cards. She says this requires precise calculations of the celestial calendar, atmospheric conditions conducive to sunspots, solar eclipses, pulsations of a dying star. Consideration of gravitational forces beyond our control, orbits in apogee, high tides.

She tells me to pick a time I'll find him spinning his plastic play-bird, splashing in his little cup. She says I must light a stick of sandalwood to soothe him. Stroke him. Coo him quiet. Feel the flutter of his heart against your fingers. Part the feathers on his breast. Hold your breath, she says, and with the scissors slice him cleanly though the keel of him to bone. There will be a heart still beating. Perhaps, at first, pulsations. A curling up of claws. But please continue. Pull back the skin. Bend back a rib. Finger in and out the ribbons of him, the miles of tangle he has been keeping secret. The gizzard full of parts of me he's swallowed: entrails, innards, stones and gravel—the clots of me for spreading out upon a plate.

More predictable than stars, she tells me.

More reliable than tarot.

More accurate than reading leaves of tea.

But instead I read the oil pan rainbows left in puddles. Instead I count off tea-rose petals on square of cotton print. I hang a mobile of the solar system, make wishes on a wired star. I save the wishbone from *el pollo*, poke through bones piled at the bottom of the pot. I read my zodiac prediction. I read the spattered papers on the floor of my Pepe's cage. My Pepe likes a headline. He likes a lovers' quarrel. He wants to hear about love unrequited, weapons recovered, names withheld.

He likes to hear me say his name in stories: My Pepe, I tell him, once you were just a *pajarito*. You were hatched high up in a tropical palm. The sky above your nest was bright with Southern constellations. The trees were full of fruit and twined with flowers. Long-tailed birds flew past you trailing the tendrils, scattering petals, singing your name.

I am singing to the radio in *la cocina*, to the spoon-beat rhythm of the Spanish ladies, the downstairs slide of a blade on a blade, and the slam-down of a lid. He sharpens his beak back and forth on the cuttlebone. He jabs at his bell. He calls me when I am at the window cooing pigeons closer and I have to watch him hanging upside down, open-winged and waving at me. I have to see him swinging with his claws around his hoop.

I have spools of thread in every color. I can match any shade of cloth you can find. I can fix a shirt gone shabby, too-tight trousers, torn *pantalones*, seam-split *camisas*. Add a pleat, make a tuck. Stitch a patch in plaids or ice cream colors. Tack a hem. Take in. Take up. Let out. I can cut, baste and buttonhole. Adjust a waistline. Work wonders with a hook and eye. I can custom-fit your wedding party: never charge for alterations, have no problem matching any color you may want in a bouquet. I have cards of lace and links of rosebuds, rows of seed pearls for beading, cardboard cones of grosgrain, embroidered bluebirds beak-to-beak. I keep strips of flocking, flounce; lengths of ruffle, yards of viscose, velvet, velveteen. I can appliqué a cuff or turn a collar; reline any coverlet, comforter, or cape. I can weave away a threadbare knee or elbow. Mend a tear so you would never notice. I can turn a spool of silver in the bobbin winder. I thread it though the guide holes, the take-up lever. I push it through the eye. I get the needle clicking and the stitches even. I sew a sky for Pepe—a lining for his cover so he has stars to sleep under at night. I keep the treadle rocking. I keep the window open. He never flies away.

He waits until it's far past the time for Señor Mantecado to be coming. He watches while I pick up scraps, pins; while I snip frayed ends, loose threads. He sees me sweep away the seed shells and put away the scissors. He sees me shut the sewing light. He peeps at me through orchids in the doorway. He flies from his perch to my sheets full of roses, eclipses the streetlight with the lift of a wing. He climbs through the buds and petals, over the patterns of brambles. "*Mi corazon*," he says, and he hooks his beak into the covers. There are places where my skin is broken. There are tiny cuts from claws.

There are places where long-tailed birds perch high up, pull open the fruit, find rows of seeds inside the sweet, bright pulp. There are places where the flowers live in trees—ruffled petals, winding stems. They weave unmended canopies, let moonlight in.

There are phases of the moons of Jupiter pressed on my ceiling. There are rings of Saturn aslant above my bed. Beyond this neighborhood a truck trimmed with electric stars plays music. It is too far off for me to listen. I can feel the beat from *la cocina* through the floorboards. I can feel his sharp mouth open. I keep the freezer full of flavors that he brings me, taste a stick of something frozen, press it into places I am nipped and bleeding. Blood dries dark on the pattern of roses. Silver ribbons spark in the caged-fan breezes. Stuck-on moons above us light the clean-swept floor.

I am watching the ceiling for the shape of him above me—the pleat and tuck of quill, of plume; the sweep of him unfolded. I am waiting for the shadows on the street-lit walls around us; for the wrap and cloak of feathers, the coverlet of wings.

Which Are Cinders

Spring these parts is peepers. Woods north, there are other ways to tell: first whipporwills, then thrashers, then those yellow ones that like to nest in thickets, hatch those babies with hairs that look like their mamas never took a comb to. Don't know their names. That spine-broke book we had with names is long gone in the fire, Sulee's book. Pa said, "See what happens when you think you know better than your own Pa knows?"

No matter. Knowing names won't help you listen. I listen. Every night been listening like Sulee used to for Pa coming—his boot hard on the board and a banged down door, and never mind no peepers. Wake up all at once, they do, just when you are thinking it's too soon for any spring. When your teeth be clattering and the cinders want poking and when you are wondering: when, oh when!—is when. I listen, but I don't let on I do. Pa wants his water on, so I hurry with my plainest face for chores while I am listening to what started while I was sleeping. Pa sits scrunch-haired at the table. He doesn't seem to hear. Not in his mind to. Pa says he knows the sound of them and makes it in his teeth, but it's a different sound than peepers. I don't like Pa's face when he shows how. I don't say, "No teeth on those peepers, Pa." He wouldn't like that sort of sassing.

I learned. Switch-taught is how. Pa cuts himself a switch and tries it out before he lays it on—swats the air like he was hunting flies but you can tell he isn't. You can hear his switch come down like far-off whistling. Like the sound of peepers. I let the sound of peepers make a song like one I sung with Sulee, like the one I made Sulee sing behind me.

I think of Sulee, but I wouldn't say, "Sulee's book," or "Sulee used to say," or "Sulee this or that," no more. Our Pa, he wouldn't like that sort of talking. Pa says, "Notions." Pa wants his water on.

You can hear above the kettle if you try to hear. I don't say, "How many peepers do you think, Pa?" But there is plenty from the sound of them, sounding like a string of *oh*s if it was writ down for you to read it. I could read it. Pa says, "A finite number." The talk he learned from books, when he had books, no doubt. Sulee used to say if you had a mind to go picking through the woods some fine night for the purpose of ciphering that number down, well then, she'd say, you'd find plenty. But I never found a one. Sulee, me—we looked in trees but never did. She dug her teeth into the bark of trees higher than deer will do. She made marks. We kept on. You might think: Just pick one that is peeping and follow it, is all. But there is no peeping when you get there. Only far off. They get far off when you come looking. Sulee's place is far off. I hear them here. I pick one peeping different from the rest. One too high like the sound the pump handle makes one cup past priming. Like the one chirp that comes one chirp higher in the sweet gum or the thicket when you say to yourself, "Not no thrasher, that," and you pitch in a stone and out flaps the same old yellow one you've been seeing all the same all spring. One to catch on to. I never can catch on. The rest come right behind in a string of peeping like a song you don't know so you follow along to catch up to. Sulee sung fine. She could sound sweet, like peepers. Pa didn't take to singing, but Sulee—she sang and sassed him anyhow, our Pa. Pa doesn't know I know that place he put Sulee last time she was singing.

Pa knows plenty.

Last spring coming when Sulee run off. Pa knew where. He picked one broke branch and followed it, is all. It didn't take him long—time enough for one book I watched burn down. I poked cinders for the picture of the yellow one when the fire was gone. You might think that paper is easy when it comes to fire. But if paper is pages, it stays together. I found the pages with the pictures of the yellow ones, but not the names. I could read where it said,

"Call: a high-pitched 'peek'; range: woods north" before the page went black along the edges. What all I was reading, waiting for Pa to catch that Sulee. For our Sulee to come back with our Pa.

Pa cut himself a switch.

I could hear Sulee make a string of *oh*s and the pump handle go twenty times past the sound of priming. Her hair was wet. She spit water, and sang a song, and then she didn't. Old Sulee could make a song from just the sound of peepers far off.

Pa made the other fire. I could see far off, but Pa didn't see me see. I never let on. In spring, before the trees have leaves to hide you, you can peep through trees. You can see a far-off fire by the sparks it shoots when someone bent and tending pokes the cinders. You can keep it in your mind where you see the sparks, and then you'll know just where it is in case you need to find it.

I know the place Pa made that other fire. I say, "Sweet gum's gone to seed by now," and Pa will let me go.

I go where the woods go north. I go where Sulee toothed the trees, and the trees lead out, but not to where our Sulee ever wants to go. Wanted to go. I know which marks were Sulee's marks and which were deer, since Sulee's ones were higher.

I know which ones were Sulee, since teeth are not easy like paper when it comes to fire. Dead fires from paper leaves book-spines black, but I can tell which ones are bones. I know which ones are teeth and which are cinders. I stand right where that fire was and listen for the peepers. I pitch a stone to where I hear the sound of the one I know chirp its one chirp higher.

But there is no chirping when you get there.

There is no peeping.

From there, you can hear far.

Aquifer

Some summers just a stick of buckeye starts you walking.

Some nights in spring a moonrise and the tug of far-off tide will be enough to steer a peeled-down switch of birch or start a wobble at the wrist. Enough to pull a branch of tupelo clean-stripped of petiole and leaf, held bud-tip down to lead you to the seep beneath the Little Dipper. Kept thumb-up at the fork to feel the pulse of sap, the sense of going somewhere—the turning of a wing of mountain ash above the water, or sinking where the pickerels face side by side into the flow and scarcely wave a fin or raise the silt. Of following behind the shadbush bloomed too early for the upstream swim of bluegill, or carrying the sprig of full-moon maple to the place the aquifer has had its fill. Seeking the spot a brook that likes to hide itself will reappear roadside, ditchwise, lit with foxfire bright as someone's lantern or camp. Finding the pool above the ford where we pitch the pebbles in: where we stir the whale-spout spray of constellations and scatter the lights outside of Orion, the stars poured from the jug beside the water bearer's feet.

Inside, something sprouting pale and spindly pushes past the cistern, climbs up the cellar stairs, and sends a tendril to the shelf where we put rows of jars of harvest years put by. The hard-pressed garden sends up only straw-grass and crab; grows only dust devils, dogbane, poorman's pepper. But still the Allegheny plum spreads a branch above the porch to border pieces of the blue-boughed view of the sea, and there it shades our days.

We count the days. We count the clouds blown by and the watch-ticks it takes to hear a stone sent down the well meet water. Days we watch the wisps of cirrus, mare's tails, but never the cumulonimbus that shifts into an anvil shape, a pileup dark and detonated. No peals are heard within the heap that rolls in thickly undersided, bolted, spooking the foal into an unbroken bucking up and down the line of fence. No foul-weather forecast or signs of precipitation. No predictions of a squall blown in from the sea. No drop in the belly of the glass-blown barometer that lifts the meniscus up the spout and sends the rock doves sheltering in eaves and evergreens, then starts the dogs snapping the strands of grass that the sickle missed around the borders of our yard.

Just skies of mackerel and buttermilk. Just dog days the noon comes calm and clabbered, birds mute, bivouacked in shady bottomland while we spend our nights beneath the Little Bear, the Dog Star.

Sunday mornings with no wind prevailing, the dogs are porched early or under, and we hear the cut-short sermon. We bow our heads, hoping for a downpour and hearing that the pharaoh's sky is overflown with locusts. We make our prayers for weather while Noah is awash somewhere and the Nile is turned to blood—dried up or undrinkable. All please rise, we hear, and comes the closing hymn: husbands hat in hand, straw and weave, and wives in bonnets for the sun or ones close-brimmed in roses of unwilting silk. While all the while they fan their fussy babies— spitting, gassy, bibbed and tuckered—little ones and converts gussied up and overheated for the most holy dunk in the spirit, for their baptismal dip.

Sunday after suppers, fresh-washed cups and plates are stacked upon the shelves, cupboards are shut, crumbs swept up. The men sit shirttailed out, talking of crops, cows, yearlings; speaking of the turning of the year; speaking of the leaves turned early. Turning the horseshoe on the springhouse door end-up in the hope that somewhere a front is holding back, or tucked in and holding tight. Hoping that the stick of chinquapin chestnut that they always gave the child they picked to hold for luck would whisper to her; would tell her what the wind might say before a rain; would pull her, point.

A catkin of mud-banked cottonwood was the child I was. "Sopping wet!" the women said who picked me up, always puddled. No matter where they set me down—on quilt or grass or hard-packed yard—crawdad and peeper always found me when they found me with my fisted sprig of chestnut or my stick of cherrywood. They took me dripping wet from the spring that no one had known was there before—but must have been—while everyone remembers how it bubbled up! The font that everyone remembers overflowing when it came my time for naming, my turn for dipping in the name of, while all the other babies stayed sleeping or sweetly screaming. Me—kicking off the swaddle from my feet, splashing hand and heel against the bowl of stone. Spilling the sacramental waters of immersion. Flinging drops into the light, as blinding as the bolt-lit firmament above the road into Damascus, leaving wayfarers saved, onlookers soaked, and me newly sanctified.

The choir hushed. Rain slowed to a patter. The drainpipe singing. Pockets emptied. Silver dollars uncollected on the plate.

Rungs of sun. Roof slats bright and steaming. Plover chipping in the bur-reed. Perch and rainbows rising near the high-water ford. Grass bent low under its starry weight.

These are days when cloud-breaks make a Jacob's ladder: after a summer squall or red sky at morning, or just before a storm moves on above the sea, above the shore I scooped out in cups to let the water find me. Where I filled my pail with shells of moon snail and sand dollar, of cherrystone and lightning whelk and limpet. Where the surf-flung stars crawl back into the waves, and tiny coil-tailed horses are upbeached and brittle, sitting finely ribbed in the sand, reined to seagrass, and winged where you might think would be a fin. Caught and corralled forever in a jar and carried home with other pieces of the sea, to be set upon the cellar shelf beside the jars of butter beans and snap. Beside the Allegheny plum put up, the coltsfoot jam put by, the store of succotash, of chard, of stoneless cherries, and the horseshoe crab left pantry-stranded and hoping for a tide.

High and low, and back I came, for a taste of the sea, for cockles and mermaids' purses. For beach plums collected in my pail and a look at the sea-logged sailors, muscled and singing a ditty. Down from the horse latitudes, up from the Dry Tortugas; out of the doldrums and Sargasso Sea: scrimshawed shipmen blown in with the sea doves, stepping lively to a sea-pipe whistle. Deckhands and seadogs set loose along the docks, unloading the oil of sperm and blue; taking on provisions and barrels of sweetwater. The coxswain is coming with coconuts and tamarind. The bosun arrives with trinkets of ebony locked in his dovetailed chest of teak. The high-water helmsman is taking his shore leave, testing his land legs, wanting me to be the storm he's riding out. And last, the foretopman, toting a sextant and taking liberties; talking of Antares and azimuth, telling celestial longitude, sidereal time. Showing me ascension and declination. Demonstrating the perpendicular to the elliptic. Horizontal parallax. Planetary positions. Finding his bearings of bow-and-beam in my bed above the porch, in the room with the blue-wide pane of plum-bordered window, above the church-towered town, above the bright road crooking hill by hill on down to the river, above the fence-lined fields sunburnt up, or rain-flattened down and framed by a bough view of the sky-blue bay.

Who will bring me a bright stick of blossoms?

Who will climb from the upstairs window? Who will step out upon the roof slats made of cedar, cut from the groves that grow along the river? Who will reach out to the bough that is slim enough for whittling?

Who will lean into the topsails of the tree, reach past the petals and roust the doves from their nightfall perch? Who will bend the branch, cut the shreddy bark, twist it round and round the way a branch won't go and give me what I need to go where the water wants me to be going?

What shall I need to be going?

A moonrise and the right branch of tupelo held not too tight. A twig of Allegheny plum or crabby apple. A wand of sandbar willow. Of horse chestnut. Of stone-fruit cherry.

Who will cut the whippy-stick of hickory to pull me to the place a spring has been keeping secrets in seepy hillside?

Who will break the stem of buckeye that will take me where I know a well is waiting to be dug, where I can tell how deep the roots of a sea-blue spruce or sycamore will reach?

Who will snap the bough of peach to say where a river leaves behind its mud-shard bed and shows me the places it would rather sleep?

Not the midshipman who wants me battened down and bedded in my bed above the porch; not the one who brings me pomegranates wrapped in paper or the spiced plums in a jar. Not the able-bodied seaman who blows into port on a gale-high wind and spins back to sea on a waterspout. Not the one who brings a brandied pear for my supper, still grown to its stem and slipped past the neck of a slim-necked bottle. Not the mariner with his pocket full of frippery and gimcrack. Not the middy swigging from the flask he filled with cups of sea at the crookedy Straits of Magellan. Not the mate who is looking for a good-time maid, or the roustabout wanting a sweet-water damsel. Not the cook who wants me keeping my cupboards and tide tables tidy-swept, or the tar or gob or crew. Not these seafarers watching out to sea from my window, waiting for a fair-sky day and a stiff breeze out and wishing for the empty spars to soon be sprouting sails.

Inside of me is something sprouting: tendril-tailed and gilly.

Inside of me is the tickly swarm of silver fishes I see flying from the spindrift spray to see me.

Sweet flag and cocklebur are hiding bluegill and minnow.

Flags are run up for getting under way; sails are full and ready.

Downriver fingerlings are swimming past where reed and bulrush bend and slipping along the bow that takes away a landlocked sailor.

Inside of me is something sprouting: coil-tailed, finned, and slit-gilled.

Upriver in me something swims the neap and spring of tides, sways with the surge of salt. Inside something is timed to the bloom of the shadbush, to an upstream swim and spawn. It swims from me too early. It is born in my bed, in sight of the windowed sea; flowing plum-tinted in the spill, in the flume of a tide turned red.

Pour it to the tide race. Spill it to the current of the ebb, before a passing shower starts the perch and rainbows rising, has them pulling at the unnamed pieces of me, mistaking parts of me for mayfly or caddis fly or freshwater damselfly or stonefly nymph. Spill it down from a jar on the riverbank. Pour it where the whirligigs will circle in the eddies and the riverbed bottom makes a bowl of stone. Turn the rocked-in pools blood-tinged and undrinkable. Empty the jar or flask of what you have been saving, or trying to save, and sanctify me. Dry me up.

First-crescent moonset will start the peepers singing.

Last-quarter rise starts the dun foal in his sleep.

Some nights in summer there is salt-tanged wind and sea smoke moving on the water. There are sea-made clouds that hold in tight the heat of the day.

The church is dark and emptied out of singing. The doxology is done, the font dried up. Sleepy dogs stay guarding at the edges of the yard, yawing and yapping at who it is comes walking through the garden where the straw-grass bends at the sickle blade; at who it is comes walking through the full-moon maples. Take along a lantern. Hang it handle-notched to a sapling to see where you are headed, to see your way along the crooks in the road. Pick the tree that's strong enough to pull you, and straight enough and green enough to bend.

A whittled length of locust or Allegheny plum will have you stepping lively. A piece of catalpa or dogwood will certainly do. It will pull you to the place to dig if you should want to sink a well or build a springhouse. It will show you the spot to wait if you would rather have the water come to fill your pail or find you. It will take you where the cress has sprouted and the morning dewfall fills a seep. It will be the way that is lit by an early-hour spray of stars set loose from a wave unraveled. A lodestar course leaning to Cassiopeia, bearing to Pegasus, steering through the constellations, flying past flying fish and keel and compass. Winging past seadove and dolphin from the depths of the heavens.

It will be a reading of meridian.

A starboard-side observation of degree and minute.

A plumb line to the vertical. A pitch and roll with the deck of a vessel, a moon-fixed correction for the aberrations of a dream.

It will be a dead reckoning past the stations of the sky where the denizens of water sleep, and a passage through the straits of the celestial sea.

Sirens, Siren

Holed up on that settee so long, losing track of time, I thought it was those sirens I was hearing. Same sort of screeching it was as last night, when I thought I was home. Where else I'd think I'd be? I reached around to Mr. Lacy's side of the bed, like I do—no, like I used to do. But he wasn't there. Couldn't be.

Lights were flashing on that wall, and I was thinking, "Our barn!" Always did worry about him puttering around so late out there with that sputtery lantern. "Fire!" I called.

But no one came.

Spied this spit-basin by the bed.

I took it and banged the bar.

"What do you want?" they said, come running.

Well, that set me wondering where they come from, and where was Mr. Lacy gone? Couldn't ask them. Couldn't let them think what I knew they were thinking.

"Is it a bad fire?" I said, like I figured it out. "Is Mr. Lacy burned bad?"

One of them smiled at the other one, seesawing her hand. He's just so-so, my Mr. Lacy, I was afraid she was saying. I'm ashamed to admit it, I began to cry.

"Hush up, now," she said. "That ambulance is going all night. Better get used to it," she said, and put this buzzer thing in my hand. "No rapping on that railing," she said.

They shut the light.

I lay there in the dark, deciphering. Feeling foolish. A foolish old thing. Mr. Lacy, he'd say, "Don't be fretting, Missus. Two of us muddleheads together will make one unmuddled."

He had a cough for a while. But didn't I believe him when he said it was the dust from the oats? Our old mare, she was way past work. We kept her as a pet, like the barn cats past mousing. Mr. Lacy, he'd wink and say, "Riding out fence-mending this morning." Old man! Riding nowheres. I knew he'd just be fetching her bucket of oats.

Winter coming looked to be his last. He kept up the chores as best he could. I'd catch him, sometimes, leaning on a hoe, breathing like he did. Or allowing lengthy pauses between axe chops. Why, just forking a wisp of hay tuckered him.

I stole out after him one morning early when he was gone too long. It was still dark, but the lantern light from under the barn door, that showed me the way. I peeked in the window. Mr. Lacy was in the stall with the mare nuzzling his pockets. That's when I figured out where my apples been going. I was set to tap on the window, calling, "Mr. Lacy, you do or don't want pies this winter?" But I saw he'd been crying. I saw they were both thinner than they used to be. Thinner than I'd like to notice.

He came back inside; it was a long time later. I was standing at the kitchen sink like I'd never been out. "Missus," he said, "I think it's time."

I didn't turn around.

I swallowed.

"Whatever you think best," I said.

I heard him in the next room, rummaging in the desk where he kept the shells.

I heard him go back out.

Ran water and banged dishes so as not to hear a thing.

When he spit blood, I called them. Had to. Told them, "Driving up, don't put that siren on." Didn't want no ruckus, you see. Neighbors needn't know.

But they did it anyway.

They don't listen.

Solstice

He likes the water hot, kept to a simmer in the iron-casted kettle
I keep hanging on the hook above the grate. He likes a loaf baking
on the bricks—white is what he says he wants—and the rest of
what's for supper ready. I set our places: the pot of what's been
cooked; the fiddleheads just picked; bread hot with blackcap jam
if I can find a bramble unpecked over by the birds.

I have a split-oak bucket that I bring him. A brush for
scrubbing. A flannel for his feet. A cake of soap sitting in the fern-
trimmed dish with one leaf missing—the place when I hold it I
keep my finger over to fool myself. Where I pretend the pattern
is unbroken and the color of shoots in early spring when these
woods have nothing else so green goes all around the edge. Soap,
I was saying—fine-grained, scented of sweetfern, made from soft
ash I sift when the firebox goes cold. Anthracite is slow. A fire
banked just right will keep a flame till morning. A chunk or two
tucked in with some still glowing is enough for bread. Bricks
make a better loaf, but I fire up the cook stove some cold nights
anyhow to see the light beneath the lids when all around the room
is dark.

I keep the damper open. Hard coal needs a draw. Sometimes it
just won't catch no matter how dry the kindling is or how much
breathing on it that I do. I give up and find stray fire on the road
or embers on the edges of the slagheap. Or if I am feeling brave
enough—the seam that's always burning on the undercliff. But
the way to there is far. Half a day without our pit-broke mule, but
Mister says I dawdle. I don't think I do. He wouldn't say so if he
saw the way I go past some parts that don't seem to want me to
be walking through, though nobody I know owns them. No signs
posted. Nothing saying, "No Trespassers." No one taking aim.

Nothing worth taking except coals along the outcrop seam that spits when it is raining, trees smoking through the cracked-off chimneys of their trunks, flying little fires into town.

Something always smolders on the hill above the pit: clumps of cinders dropped from somebody's scuttle, flow-in windfall, spark-lit sticks of shagbark not quite caught. Someone passing by will stop to stamp a little fire out. Someone kicks on snow or dust or whatever's in the road, depending on the season. Black souls and hot feet the preacher says we've got. Hellfire metaphor, he calls it. What he says we all need a good dunking in the river for; what we need John the Baptist for, unfastening our sandals and taking sinners like us under.

He says: forgive us our debts. Forgive us our trespassers. Deliver us from sleeping through what you'd think everyone would want to stay awake for, not nodding off like my Mister. Not head-down nearly in the hymnal like every other Mister his wife will bring along the only day he doesn't have to wake before the hoot-owl shift will finish. Before the cable lifts the cage that loads him on and drops him back into the dark.

Mornings it is songbird song that wakes me—our caged one answering the ones outside that winter over. They light along the chimney rim and whistle down the stovepipe. They wait for heat. I stir the ash and I hear them singing. I sift the clinkers through the grate. I listen while our caged one holds himself slim-winged, head tilted up, singing up and down the scale the same the upright does in Sunday service. We never take a window seat. We never sit in sunlight coming through the colored picture-glass—the one that shows Him stepping from the Jordan River, the water dripping over, the Spirit like a dove rose up and ringed with fire. Mister is unused to light. Unused to seeing something just straight on, not flickering in the firelight he's used to scrubbing by, or in the lamplight from his cap. Unused to singing that isn't from a songbird caged-hooked to his belt, is what I think these Sundays when he won't follow printed notes, just sits and squints

70

at hymnal pages lit too bright. We slide down the bench. He likes the aisle—a fast escape, he says, a getaway when the preacher tells us: Go in peace.

I never like to go. I like the painted-on dove hanging above the pulpit. I like the sprigs she holds of something she found growing when the waters were receded. When at last she found a place to rest her foot: "And lo," they said, "her mouth did hold the leaf plucked off." A fern of sorts, it must have been, a fiddlehead uncurling in some soggy spot the day they set her loose. Something bright and green she must have spied against the all-black mud. I find them where the shagbark makes it shady. And all along the undercliff—the seam that heats the spring. That fire kills some things right off; some things need the char. Choke, for one, and coltsfoot need a burned-out patch to sprout. And blackcaps need a seared-off place where I find songbirds pecking berries. I catch them red-beaked and too busy to see my snares or me, squat-down in the Larkspur, watching for the one who lands without looking, claw-caught and tight in my net midflight. I find them when these woods get quiet. I wait until my almanac says the equinox is near and catch the ones who stay to wait the season out. I wait until some morning I see Mister hook our one last caged-up songbird to his belt. I lie in wait. I wind the snare thread on my finger, ready. I stay ready. Hid out in tall stems, petals ruffled by the wind rising from the river bluffs, moving clouds high up enough to still look clean against the sky. I tell the one that soon will be our last one left to look at the sky, while I unloose the fine net from its wing-sprout spaces, untangle from its feet. It toe-holds to my finger. It peeps but I say hush. I am careful of the claws. I am careful of the wings. It will not need its wings. I fold them flat to hold it. The first frost comes and I find the ones who winter over, scratching in the white-rimed grass. Splashing where the seam along the undercliff melts down the snow.

That seam, they say, runs longer than nobody knows how long.

71

Wide nearly to the bluffs where the river going under cools it, turns bitter, sends the fish away to deeper water. Deep to where the forest that it's made from still lies buried. I bring along the scuttle, fill it to the top with live coals enough for baking and some left over. I try that kindling one last try before I cheat with fire ready-made. And don't you know: it always comes. That teaches you. My gram taught me bread, but bread will teach you nearly as well: waiting while the snowmelt water wakes up the yeast, punching down, pushing it along the board, waiting while it rises. Lift the cloth to peek and that just slows it. Watched pot is what they say, but I say: Loaf. I say: Dough. What I get busy doing when the ground makes a thunder you can feel up through your feet. When the dishes rattle in the rack until the fern-trimmed one before it chipped slides off what seems like slow, circles on its rim, ringing, then claps itself down quiet. First comes the shift-change whistle. Then the breaker crashing that no one took a notice of before will stop. Quitting time? I wonder, until I hear the steeple bell. A wife within the sound of it sets whatever she was scrubbing down to soak. Leaves what she was hanging still flapping on the line. Forgets her pail of blackcaps in the bramble she just stood picking in and heads for home.

Home, is what my Mister says ahead of time: Go home. Stay at home. Wait for word. He says: No sense in getting in the way, watching for the men when they start coming up. A wife out walking within the sound of it turns around. Nods to people passing on the road. Other women going home or heading down. Preacher with his Bible arm-tucked in. Folks sitting in their windows looking out. Pushes through the gate that never closes unless you notice, past the pit-broke mule broke loose but not leaving. Past the cage left hanging in the shagbark where she set a spare songbird for seeing sky, getting air. Fast-stepping out any little flown-in fires or hay strands smoldering. Stops for a second on the front porch step. Heads straight to the shelf where she keeps her baking pans without taking off her hat. Lifts down her sack of flour. Picks up her bone-handled knife. Levels off a cup. Sifts. Sifts. Watches flour dust sprinkle down onto a plate. Shakes out the screen, the little stones that don't get through. Lets her mind settle. Makes a mental list. Tells herself the things a wife will tell herself. Finds the little chores she should be doing. Refolds a quilt. Fluffs the pillow on the front-room bed. Considers flowers for the front-room table. Considers that a sick room really isn't without flowers. Wonders if it is spring enough for flowers: Speedwell she remembers seeing somewhere. Harbinger-of-spring inside the churchyard. Day lilies along the fence. Solomon's Seal, Jack-in-the-pulpit, and wouldn't sprigs of birdsfoot trefoil look pretty if all else fails? Finds oil enough in the front-room lamp. Fiddles with the chimney glass, trims the wick. Lets her spine-broke Bible fall open in her lap, so pages turn without her touching: wedding date written on the flyleaf. Pen-and-inked picture of rings tied with ribbon. Flat-pressed petal. Sweet-fern bookmark. Favorite verse. Loaves and fishes. Potluck supper invitation. Scrap of paper with hymnal selections. Carols of praise. Wings of joy. Song of Solomon. Jeremiah. Lamentations. Envelope for the widows' fund. Contributions. Late donations. Lets a page turn over: the part about Him riding on a mule into Jerusalem; the people with the fronds of palm. The part about the lilies of the field; the songbirds who sow not. Sits until the lamp goes out and finally turns up the wick. Finds a favorite chapter, puts her kettle on in case. Catches herself in the mirror at the sink. Undoes the ribbon on her hat. Sets it on the front-door hook. Pulls open the latch. Looks out from the front-porch step: last-quarter moon where the almanac says it would be; gate wide open; pit-broke mule pointed out but not going; songbird still hanging in the shagbark. Not a sign of stirring. Not a note of singing. Not a sign of someone coming up the road. Lets a page turn over: the part about the angel at the sepulcher; the stone that rolled away; the women waiting by the tomb. Waits for word. Does whatever needs to be done.

I test for doneness. Soap needs a knife-curled piece touched on the tongue to test, but bread is different. Bread takes a finger tapping out a sound on top. Mister says it comes the same as the rapping of a shovel on the roof-rock with coal dust sifting down between the slats. The sound you find in tunnels for a fast escape from, where loose rock hides out of reach above the roof-prop timbers that creak and pitch with miles of earth-shift weight. The places that you can slide in the flat end of a pick. I slide the bone-handled knife along the sides. That's the other way to tell, my gram told me—the way it shrinks along the graniteware pan she handed me down before she died. Harder, is what she said, no matter how hard I had to push my hands into the dough along the floury board. Long past baking, she told me from her bed, holding up her hands, her rings stuck on below her knuckles knotted up from scrubbing, and me pretending mine would never. Me pretending any ring I wore would always budge so easy off my finger, slip right off with just a dab of soap. Twist right off above the bone that keeps it on. The things a girl will tell herself. She could tell by the color of the crust and finally by smell when what she was seeing turned too dim to see. I never got as good. I set all my ones burnt black or never risen out for snaring songbirds. One loaf they never even touched. Perched on top without so much as pecking. Mistook it, likely, for a stone. I take it in a muslin cloth; turn it out onto a plate. I keep it covered for the heat. The cloth is clean. I don't know how. Sometimes the ones I pull in off the line before a rain look like they never did see soap, unless I scrub with snowmelt water. Unless I skip windy days when the slagheap dust gives the clouds a dark shimmer if the sun shines this way just so. Solstice is still months away, the almanac says. The sun, it says, supposing to be a slant closer, but it doesn't ever seem it's coming. It seems I always will wake up with songbirds singing before the light. Before I feel my feet cold along the floor and set his boots beside the fire. I climb back in, lean over, and tell him, "Time." I tell him, "Ready." I say I have breakfast ready.

And later—some nights it is much later—I say I have dinner on the stove. That pit-broke mule that never leaves our yard will bray and stamp when he is coming down the road. When I hear him pulling closed the gate that won't unless you notice. I hear the sound his foot makes on the front porch step. The sound the step makes from his weight.

Our sheets are white. I scrub with snowmelt water.

I make a fine-grained soap, sweetfern put in for scent.

I smell the put-out fires. I smell the mud, the smell of river going under on his clothes. The water there is bitter. I want to taste the river. See the sky up through the water. Feel the weight of river rise above me. Feel the weight of him above me. Tell him: ready. Feel the timbers loose and shake. Feel the shift of weight. I want to see the men come up.

I have seen the pit-broke mules come up. I have seen them turn their tall ears to the creaking cable of the cage, to the sounds the men make to keep themselves steady, standing at the withers of the mules, singing what the mules know the sound of when it crashes to the top. Praise Him all creatures here below, they sing when I have seen those mules—old, white-muzzled beneath the dust, pit-blind from the years of pulling far below the light. I have seen them blink away the black dust in their lashes, stamp and shake the shag of coats kept long by everlasting winters of the pit. I have seen the fingers of the men held crooked around the halter rings, shielding the eyes of mules from skies not seen since foaled. Waiting for the cage to haul them up. For the shining sky to meet them at the top. For the sun not to smite them by day nor the moon by night, by moon-bright night.

I have seen the songbirds coming up, turned loose to find their way out from a tunnel. I have seen them burning in the air. I have watched their scorched, unfettered flight.

I fill the bucket up. I bring the brush for scrubbing. I bring our fine-grained soap. Unfasten the laces of his boots. Put the flannel on the place where he will put his feet. I know the way to fool myself, pretending there are things I must be doing. I set the places. Bring the bread. Jam in a dish. Bone-handled knife. The loaf uncovered over. The kettle will be ready. I listen for when he says: ready. I lift the split-oak bucket. I pour the water over. There is fire on the grate. The lamp is on the table. The wick is turned down low. The light inside the stovepipe. The flame inside the hearth. The halos of the lids. The hush and spit of anthracite. The Bible on the shelf. The bucket by the handle. My finger on the rim. The ring below the bone. The smell of sweetfern soap. He turns himself around: the drip and spark of water. He hands me up the brush for me to finish. I have his back to do, the place he cannot reach.

Harder is what he tells me, no matter how hard.

I press the bristles to the soap and start to scrub.

A Comfort in the Stones

The slate, the stair, the flight below the parapet, are not, I tell myself, the polished slope and sag they seem, the wearing down that comes from countless steps—our steps—upon the stone.

The marbled way into the nave, the tiles of terra cotta to the gate, are not the leveled thoroughfares laid down for our walking.

The stones we step upon are cobbles of the ancient street, but not so hard, and not so cruel upon the foot. Not even where the flag along the cloister walk is sharp, known to pinch in places amaranth and rockweed widens out a crack, or cut where castings of worms will push the broken pieces up. Besides, this weight is just a prayer, a burden of the heart, is not some square-hewn beam, lashed to the shoulder, given to resting in the grooves made by the way the stones were laid down end to end. A weight given to pulling one back, scraping on the stairs that one would have to take to get to anywhere within the walls, or Herod's gate, or any hill without. One must walk head-down along the stones. One must hold the book. One must speak the word, keep the word upon the tongue just long enough to count each seed, pierced and strung, before it slips along its strand between the fingers, or long enough to feel a pebble underfoot press against the skin where the sole is weak. Where the feet will stray along the walk. One must take a comfort in the stones. One must keep confinement of the eyes upon the page, not lifted for the dip and wing of dove or angel passing over, shadowing the walk or flitting in the hips and buds of roses. One must watch for where the flag-laid path will take a turn along the row of hedge and the hermit's garden—gray, blue, blue, then red, then blue again before the bend of briar rose that hangs too full below the bower at the well and catches at the wimple and the veil. One must know the pace and count of someone else's walking, see the kick of cloth just above Crucita's ankle—Crucita's ankle bared below the hem, one stone, one brick ahead. One must hold the book. One must move the lips according to the step along the stones and know the stones are often wet on winter mornings where the slate is black, and where the flag has turned the color of His blood. One must breathe the verse appointed to the hour, according to the hour, bear a witness to the verse. One must listen for the bell. Her foot is brown. Crucita's foot is brown from sun and hoeing up the garden—days I have seen her hitch the layered fall of serge out of the dirt, tuck it in the cincture at the waist. Higher there the leg is pale, slim-boned—I can but assume how white it would be, I can only think it so, of course not having seen.

In and out a verse.

The slightest blue of vein, the tint of cloister flag.

The fingers set the hasp that keeps the hermit's gate.

The hum of final prayer is heard behind the thatch.

The fingers turn the page.

The verse, the step, the falling seed all fit the cadence of the waking heart.

Winter mornings when we wake we are in step to the stone. We are knees upon the straw. There are words to be spoken at the tolling of the stone-tamped bell. There is ice on the basin by the bed. But not so cold as it may seem, I tell myself—this water carried clasp-handed to the body after the ice is broken and the drops are free and falling, unstrung in my fingers and not so cold upon the breast.

It is, instead, it seems, a blessing: the glaze of it upon the briar and the thorn, making bones of twigs and limbs that break by noon and lie along the walk with the melt of winter mornings shining in the hollows of the stones.

We walk the stones with spade and pail, with sickle blade and fork. We hasten to His work. We turn the soil along the wall. We lift our hems to carry off the hips of roses, gather up the smoothest stones and set them in a string of stones along the border of the walk. We pitch the hay into the paddock. We lift the settled hen above her nest without her waking, fling the millet seed inside the coop and dovecote. We find the hoof-split hollows where the lambs have stepped, their dung beside the trough, the wisp of fleece caught on a stick of straw or thorn.

We do not have the straw on which the Magi knelt.

We do not have a thorn saved from the briars that He wore.

We do not know what notes of praise were heard the day that she was chosen, or in her heart what voice—what bird—was singing.

We do not have a vial of precious milk He suckled at His birth or the reed that someone set inside a sponge, held up to Him along the square-hewn beam so He might sip and wet His lips.

We have only the stone He picked out of the road and bade them to cast forth, or one of many that they let fall from their hands and left Him with the woman where she knelt, where she hid herself away in the folds of His garment where her hands were clinging.

We do not have a snippet of her hair—the veil and fall of it she hung upon his feet, and sometime later sold off strand by strand as she had sold herself.

We never had a fragment of His bone—no metatarsal or bit of heel broken by the hammer and the new-forged nail.

I have never held her foot or ankle in my hand—only as a penance when steadied on my knee to pour the water in the basin over.

We do not have the basin that they used to wash the body.

We do not have the jar of spice they used for scent, or the shards of the urn in which the oil was kept for His anointing.

We do not have the vial of tears that Lazarus cried when he was wakened from the tomb and they called him to come out.

We do not have the pebbles that they placed inside the hollows of his face.

We have only the penance of the rose: the flick of branch stripped clean of bud and leaf, the thorn against the flesh.

We have only the penance of the stones.

We have the word to speak along the stair, the slate.

What we see from out the casement on the stair is not, I tell myself, the pastured hills, the fen, the pond. What we see along the sill and slotted window of the cell is not the hedgerow or the hermit's lair, is not the paddock for the lambs. The shadow at the wall where we have turned the garden over is not a darkness of the loam—the place the shovel rests to press and lean the foot. It is, instead, the stir and push of soil beside the tomb, made by the wedging open of the heavy door where the sod grows over. Where the moss fills in the cracks, coaxed on by the drip and seep along the slab of rock. Did Lazurus lift his head from the pillow of the stone and see the crack of light along the door? Did he think he had awakened from some reverie or dream? Did he stagger to the light in mold and tatters? Did he weep to see the soil beneath his nail, to see the hand that he had lifted in the dark to feel where he was laid upon the earth and stones, to dig his fingers in the wall, and finding where he was in his awakening, did he weep and let the worm fall from his mouth? Did he step squinting to the light, shielding his sight from the sight of his body, smelling the taint of his flesh as it fell from the ruin of his body, as the wrap of the gravecloth unraveled at his feet, and did he thank Him then for that—for all of that—or did he kneel and curse His name?

We keep His name upon our lips. We coax the name from where are hearts will keep it hidden.

This we keep hidden:

The hands within the sleeves when not attending to His work.

The reliquary set in the wall of the nave.

The nest of the dove.

The wing of the bird that flew from her heart.

The wing of her shoulder where the bone forms a blade—this I best believe it so, would only think it so, of course, not having seen.

This we keep hidden:
The head beneath the drape of veil.
The breast beneath the rough-made cloth.
The book in the sleeve when not open to the word.
The nights Crucita waits along the stair outside my door and lifts the latch.
The nights the word, the prayer, is kept upon the lips.

We say the verse we know according to the bell. We say we know Him by His body of which we eat. We know Him by the wound, the blood of which we drink. We ask to know the way, that He will know us at His door. The fingers turn the page. The hands hold up the book. The lips press to the page before it closes. The word is kept between the covers. I put the string of seeds to mark the place. Crucita lifts her hem above her heel; slides the cloth along her leg; undoes the cincture at her waist. Her fingers stray across my breast. My lips will part against the breast. My tongue will press against the bud.

We let the seeds fall from the book.

We ask Him for the path; for the unfolding of the petals; for the lifting of the dove without her waking.

We ask the stones upon the hills: please fall on us; we ask the Lamb to cover us.

We ask Him for the dark, the sight of stars above the sill, the fall of night to keep us hidden.

This we keep hidden:
The rough-rocked way behind the hedge where we must step.
The shale that keeps the hem out of the mud.
The hermit in his lair; the thatch, the fen, the door.

It must be in some prayer or dream, I think, he hears me call him to come out. And he comes when I call him to come out: dim-eyed, he is, at his hovel door, cloaked in lambskin and morning light; his head wreathed round in vines where birds still nest amidst the thorns and buds of roses, a ligature of briars at his wrist.

The hermit's hand, I tell myself, is not so crooked and callused as it seems, unfastening the hasp that holds the gate before the hut; reaching for the basin that I bring, that I fill with hips of roses; reaching for the water in the jar so he might sip. The hermit's finger, as he holds it to my lips, is not, I tell myself, the soil-black nail that moves along my skin, below the clavicle, under the veil. It is, instead, a hand once broken where the palm was pierced and hammered to the square-hewn beam. Where the seeds of sacred blood are spilling from His wound, free and falling to my lips where I am drinking of his body. Where He pulls me to His body, to the coarse-fleeced hair of His loins; pulls me to His hips, the holy bones and hollows of His belly; pulls me to the hot-forged nail: pieced, pure, and hammered.

We do not have the hammer.

We do not have the hammer or the saw or the plane He used to shape the cypress they had taken from the hills and squared that timber to a rough-hewn beam. We do not have the lathe, or nail, or His carpenter's level.

We do not have the lots they cast to win His cloak.

We did not hear the cock that crowed on the morning of His death while He waited in the garden.

Did He wish the cock would cease and the hen would go on sleeping?

Did He wish the stands of cypress on the hills could keep Him hidden?

Did He ask to walk along the hills, through flocks of grazing lambs, and carry one along His shoulders, slung belly to His neck the way the shepherds do, His hands around the shining hoof? Did He ask to walk once more in orchards of the fig and palm, through groves of olives in the garden?

We do not have the cast-off stones of the olives in the press.

We do not have a feather of the carrion bird, hunch-winged and patient on the square-hewn beam, waiting for the pull of His flesh and the rot of His body.

We have only the stone that He found along the garden walk, on the morning of His death, amidst the mustard-weed and myrrh, or hidden in the spikenard and wingstem herb where He knelt and held it: smooth in His palm, weighted in His hand, and it was wet with the dew; and it was cold with the morning.

One can only think it so, must only think it so—of course not having seen; of course not having been there on that morning.

Morning, and the garden stones are wet. The snow melts on the flag where we have walked. We walk along the line of hedge and clip what catches at our heads, or creeps too close beside the path. We listen for the pealing of the bell and we hear, instead, a song of praise. We hear it in the mouth of the hedgerow bird; we hear it the murmur of the dove. We bend and drop the seed into the rows, break the clods of earth with hoe and spade. We turn the dung of lambs into the garden loam and leave it for the worm to do its work.

We have a verse for working in the garden.

We have the words for taking to our knees each night upon the straw, a verse for waking in the morning, and one for wearing down the stone. Crucita walks one verse, one seed, ahead along the flag, and stops before the tiles that turn into the gate. The briar holds her at the hem until she frees it from the thorn, and starts, again, the pace according to the stones set in their places.

The slate, the flight, is polished by the slide of hem along the stair; the rough-shaled way along the hedge is worn down by our walking. We know the hidden path along the fen, and where the mud is cold and deep.

We know the places where the stepping stones are shards beneath the foot: sharper than the stony hoof or sickle blade. Cutting on the quarried edge where moss fills in to hide my blood.

A Tendency to Be Gone

This, late the stones come up. This time of year the ruts freeze over. I can see them from my window. I keep myself away from the road.

I keep a knife tucked in my pocket. I like the blade wrapped tight in floss to keep from sticking. It is bad luck to lay a knife down blade-side up. It is bad luck to lose some kinds of stones. It is bad luck to save the stone that breaks your window or to lose the one you like to keep for sharpening a blade. I have a tendency to lose things. I have a tendency to let some things I like to keep fall though my pocket. It is lies you tell if you keep your knife stuck blade-side down inside your pocket. It is lies you hear if you climb in through a window and then leave by the door. It is whispering you hear if you stay low and listen near the hinges. I know a spell to quiet whispering.

I know a spell to still a voice inside a pillow.

I know a spell to stop up bleeding with the floss of milkweed, to keep fresh milk uncurdled, to close a wound with strips of willow bark or clear a rheumy eye.

It is a bad sign to come upon creatures dead-born in a hollow, their eyes still sealed, their ears still folded over. It is worse to touch the one born with a caul, to put your hand where you will not see your hand: around a stick poked down a burrow, slid along the sill of a doorway, or slipped into a box you like to keep locked up.

It is a right charm to count backwards on your fingers to keep you free from fits, from fancies; to keep you safe from someone coming up behind you when you are looking down through skim-ice to the water; to keep the water from filling in a hole you might have dug.

It is a strong spell to take the sheet a child—a boy—was born on, burn it on a willow fire, blow the ashes on a milkless mother: her breasts and lips, her hair.

I let them take my hair.

I hang it in the willow.

I let them tug the strands of me from willow twigs, take me in their beaks and feet, fly me through the air. I watch them pull me through their nests to spin a tighter weave.

I watch out for the boy.

I watch out for him through the cracks along the hinges. He comes along not watching out but catching sparkflies in his hands or talking to the dog. I think there is a dog. I think I hear the boy. I keep nights listening at the door in the room I keep dark. I have no candles. I burn twigs of willows. I put twigs of willows where the door had hinges, where I listen for him breaking sheets of skim-ice on the ruts.

Creaking birches.

Cracking branches for a stick peeled down to poke loose the leaves in the narrows where the water empties out. Where darning needles touch the foam-wet stones and the water noise is whispers, hushing, talking, voices, voices, lies told.

The water there is clear. It is a cure.

It is a cure for voices to pound the blooms of swallow-wort into a powder, to stir the powder into the coldest water from the narrows with a blade-sharp stick of willow, to pour the water back and forth between two white-glass cups and drink it through a cloth.

Try not to lose the stick of willow.

It is a cure for losing to cut hair from a boy who does not know his mother, to tie the locks in bunches up with blades of blue-eyed grass. Use the grass instead of thread. Use a knife to cut, not scissors.

Try not to use a knife with a rusted blade.

Try not to lose a boy.

It is a cure for losing to take the needle used to sew a gown for someone you had to bury. Put the needle in the footprints of someone you want to find. Try not to lose the needle.

This is a charm for finding: look in ruts for a pushed-up stone that favors what it is you want to find, and rub the stone against your lips while counting forward the numbers of your hairs you can pull out with one hand.

Try not to count such stones.

Try not to kiss such stones when you push them cold against your lips.

It is a cure for losing to crush a leaf of milkweed with your foot when you are walking. Providing milkweed is not what you are looking for. Providing you have not been walking far.

It is a cure for being lost to save the dirt and hair you sweep from inside a kennel. Keep this tucked inside your pocket; sprinkle this into your footprint on the path and pick which way you want to wander. Providing that you want to wander.

It is a cure for wandering to scrape a knife on four corners of a table and cut in half a wren egg boiled hard. This charm will keep a dog beside you if you feed it to the dog. This charm will keep a boy. But do this without talking of a boy. Without thinking of a boy.

This is a cure for thinking.

This is a charm for catching a boy.

It might be a charm for catching spiders.

It is bad luck to chase away spiders or to put your foot on spiders should you see them in the doorway.

Come in, come in.

When you leave, leave by that door.

Come in. Please do.

Please come away from the window. The glass is broken in the frame. Please do not touch the shards, the upstuck blades, the stone that flew in and stays on the sill. I will set a pane of skim-ice in that window when the weather is colder. Come in.

I will not keep you. I will not keep you in.

This is the box I keep water in a bottle in. This is the cork I use for a stopper.

This is the lock. This is how I stop the keyhole up and carry the key in my pocket the number of days there are eggs I count in the nest blown down. I need to mend this pocket.

Come in, come in.

Watch where you step when you step through the door.

There may be spiders. This is a spider's web.

This is my bed. This is a sheet. I keep this sheet from touching the floor. This pillow is filled with milkweed floss. Those are not eggs you see on the pillow—just stones that could be taken for eggs.

Please do not take the stones.

Please do not touch the blade.

Please hand me down the basket. It is a wicker basket. It holds any stones I might find with faces. It holds the foot of a crow. That is my hair that the claws try to hold. I will not hold you here. Here is a cup of the water. Here is a chair, here is a chain. Sit down. Take a chair. Please do. I will not keep you. I promise not to keep you.

If you do not keep a promise you must put your shirt on backwards while you hold a stone resembling the person and say, "Sorry, sorry." You must drink a gill of good whiskey, if you have it. You must, to mend a broken promise.

That is a broken chair.

Sit here.

Please sit here.

That chair will wobble.

It has a tendency to wobble. It has a tendency to walk across the room and brace the door.

The seat is wicker.

That is not a chair to stand on.

I try standing on that chair to see the spiders. They make their nests in the corners of the doorway. Have you seen a thread of silk stream from the belly of a spider? Have you seen the hole in her belly where the thread unspindles? She spins a web each night to catch the sparkflies. She mends her web each morning.

I mend my ways each morning.

I see webs with sparkflies sewn tight in. Bitten still by spiders, but still not dead where they are hanging and hushed up in broken threads.

Once I was good at sewing when I had a steady hand.

Never put your hand high up along a doorway where you cannot see your hand. Never say you're sorry when you see a frost-ring moon. I see the boy from the doorway before I wake up. I wake up in the morning with my hair unspun, with me wiping my mouth of foam, with this room tipped over and the chairs walked to different places than they were. I am wobbly on my feet but I can stand. I can still stand on that chair if my feet stay on the corners and I am careful not to put my feet where the wicker punched through. Where I feel a hole against my body. Where I feel as if I am going down a hole when I am sitting on that chair and a baby could come through when I am on that chair and I may open up.

If you want to keep a baby inside you, find a stone shaped like an egg; tie it with your hair; put it on your pillow.

If you want to keep a boy beside you, find a stone shaped like a boy; wash it in the narrows; push it up inside you.

But it must not be the stone that you were looking for. You must just come upon it. If you come upon a creature born late in the year and killed of frost, you can tell how long it has lain there dead by looking at its eyes. But first count forward out loud as many days until a moon first-quarter. First look around for the mother. Be sure the mother of the creature is gone. The mother will be gone. Such a mother has a tendency to be gone, has a tendency to wander when she knows it is cold as the air is. When she holds it close to her breast and lips. Touching with lips can tell cold before fingers. Touch it if the mother is given up and gone. Bend down. The belly will be white. The back will be brown. Lift the lip up at the side with your finger. Look in the mouth. It is too early for a tooth. Such a tooth—if you find one when you are not looking—is a charm as strong as a child's lock of hair. Look at the hair where it hangs above the eyes. Eyes will be bright on a day it is not dead long. Seeds will be bright on your palm if you shake out a pod in your hand. Try not to count them. Blow them away over water for luck. Blow on the fur, on the hair, while you hold it in your hand, down to where you will see where the skin is. The skin will be white if you wait long enough for the eyes to stop shining. What is dead still can see until the eyes pinch over.

Have you seen a possum play dead with her eyes pinched over?

Have you seen her fall down stiff, her legs up, mouth open?

Have you seen the pocket in the skin of her belly? She keeps babies in the pocket. Look inside her when she is sleeping. Roll her body over. You can touch one. If you hold one too long it goes cold in your hand. If you wait until morning she will wake up from pretending. She will stand up wobbly. She will shake herself off and lick her belly. She will bend down, look in. She cannot count one missing. She will run. She will leave you with the cold thing still in your hand. You can keep it a while in your pocket.

This is what I keep in my pocket: the key to a box; the sweepings from the floor; the stone with a face.

I push it far down in the slit of my pocket. I have a tendency to lose things.

This is a charm for losing:

Take a bottle that has lost its stopper.

Take a cord from a creature dead-born.

Twist the cord around the bottle—the neck of the bottle—as many times as there are links in any chain you may happen to have.

Keep the bottle in a box you have a lock to. Keep the key in your pocket. Stick it deep in your pocket where you will find it.

Providing that you want to find it.

This also cures mouth-foaming and fits—providing the person has never fallen through the ice or into a hole that fills with water.

Stones fall in the water where the skim-ice is thin. The milk was thin on the front of my shirt. I thought it was water. This I do remember. I remember what lives near the water: honeysuckle, selfheal, foam flower. Here is what lives near the narrows: sticktight, mother blight, broom. Here is what grows by the road: stonecrop and meadow rue.

Cut blue-eyed grass with a stone-sharp blade.

Fetch baby's breath in a stopperless bottle.

This will make a dull eye brighter. This will make a dull blade sharp. This will quiet a baby crying.

What can you hear if you lift the lip up at the side of the mouth and you listen? There is the sound of crying and a mother hushing. There is the sliding sound of scissors opening. There are words that may be: "sorry, sorry"—but to make up words from sounds—this is just a fancy.

What can you hear if you listen near a burrow or a hole you have dug? There are creatures asleep this late in the year. There are things still stirring that you had to bury. There are stones too sorry to come up.

What can you hear if you push bottleneck deep in the mud? There is the whispering when the wind goes over. There is the sound of a spindle. There is the sound of the sweep of a broom.

Keep any sweepings you may happen to have.

Knot any thread you may happen to keep.

Save any stones with the face of a boy.

I have a tendency to pick up stones. Stones have a tendency to hide, to shy away, to take on the face of a boy. Please take down the basket.

That is where I keep my sewing, where I keep the thread, the stones, a strip of white birch bark to hold a needle. That is the wing of a darning needle. Those are the eggs from the nest of a wren. Could you please set these down on the chair? Can you see how the curve in this stone is his cheek?

This hole is where his mouth goes. This hollow is for eyes. At first they are closed when you first hold him. When you wait for him to stop pretending. You will wait for his eyes to open. You will want to say, "Sorry, sorry."

I pretended to be sleeping when I heard them say, "Sorry." They threw away my basket. They bent the birch down. The bark was split. The nest was broken. With my ear held down I could hear them say, "Hush." With my mouth held open, with them pushing through the foam. With my fingers in the leaves. What had fallen from the willow were frost-stiff blades. I could feel the twigs of willow, the stems of nettle. A needle. A knife. A peeled-down stick pushed up a burrow. Stuck in the narrows where the water empties out. I could feel me roll over. I could see the wicker-weave of branches when I looked up. I could see their stones for faces. The sky behind them. The sky above me. The birds skim over. They tug at my hair. There goes a darning needle. Their wings are clear. Here comes a crow. A wren. A seed of milkweed the wind catches by its floss. I can see where my basket has fallen.

Please pick it up.

Put back the stones, but do not count them.

No need to count them. No need to count the needles. I keep the needles stuck in bark. I keep that thread knotted. I keep that wing of darning needle for looking through to see the branches. I save that empty egg for sweepings. It is a safe place for sweepings, providing you have no pocket. Or your pocket needs mending.

These are things I must be mending: the wicker chair; my seam-split shirt; the places willow blades have torn.

These are places I should be sewing over: my empty pocket; my unsealed ear; my bottom-slit belly. The place to push a stone inside me. The parts of me for closing up.

This late in the year the ruts are icing over.

There are pockets full of blades.

There are furrows.

There are leaves stuck in the narrows making nests between the stones. Filled with twigs. Shreds of bark. Eggs of foam. What the water likes to sweep.

Where the skim-ice makes a see-through ledge along the banks and I watch the black water slide under. I watch until dark. I find my doorway by the sparkflies caught by spiders.

Have I told you I have no candles?

I have no spell to make the narrows open up.

I have no spell to make a boy.

Spell a name backwards in the mud with a stick and someone you spell will come. Spell a name out loud in your sleep and you will find a stone with the name. Say you are sorry in your sleep and the face at your window will come in.

Do you make any sound in your sleep?

Do you know the sound that a wrong wind is saying? The sound of broom straws sliding on the floor. The sound of a thread undone from a spindle. The whispers in the narrows. The noise in your pillow. Whatever it tells you.

There is nothing I have told you.

Tell a dog to stay and it will stay if you tell it. You can tell a boy to stay—but there is no telling. Tell a blade to stay sharp while you cut into an egg. Eat with that knife while you talk to the dog. Never keep a dog on a broken chain.

Break three willow twigs if you see a moon some morning. Do this in the morning, at noon, at midnight. Make your shirt a pouch in front by holding up the hem. Put them in. Carry them home. Light each one with a candle—if you have a candle. Touch any wounds you may happen to have with the end of the twig. The wounds will close up. The bleeding will stop. Do this if you have a tendency towards bleeding.

I have a tendency towards bleeding.

Cold water on cloth will take out blood.

This cloth was a sheet. This stain is rust. This is the place that tore. Some tears you cannot see. Some wounds need sewing, but my thread is knotted up.

I keep a crow's-foot comb for unknotting my hair, for smoothing out my hair when it comes unspun. I pull it from the claws. I pull it through my needle. Hair is fine for sewing when the thread you have is knotted, when you have a sheet you need to mend. This is the sheet that a boy was born on. Boys have a tendency for getting lost. I have a tendency to lose things—but I have told you. A tendency to lose what I am telling.

Willows tell the leaves they are sorry when the moon has a ring. When they turn to the color of a rusted blade. The color on a stone mashed too hard against your lips. The color of floss from a knife wiped of blood or a sheet soaked through to the leaves blown down. I count them in the narrows. They stop the water up in the spaces between stones.

Sometimes the floss of milkweed will not stop up bleeding.

I see the seeds sleep in the floss when the pods are dry and seam-split open. Sometimes I try to close them shut. Sometimes I try to count what is left, before they hide, before they are leaving. Before they float in where the pane is broken and fly out through the door.

They blow along the road. I keep myself away. I keep out of the wind that makes whispering near the door. It unravels the webs of spiders. I have no spell to mend them. It is dark in the doorway without sparkflies.

It is cold near my window.

Water freezes in the bottle; the eggs become stone. The nest is unspun and broken. The birch is bent lower.

The twigs I keep for candles will soon be burnt down.

The stone I keep on the sill is all that is not borne away.

Overland

There is talk, now, of the Paca Bunta.

There is much to-do made each night of procedures to repel them; much ceremony in the placing of the boughs of stinkwood beyond the light of night-watch fires; in the sprinkling of stinkwood ash out past the perimeter of our sleeping places— the little hollows that the porters and the bearers have scooped out in the earth, shaped to fit the shoulder and the crest of the hip. There is much attention to the spreading out of the skins of springbok, the hides of wildebeest and zebra—the bedding down beside the tent where Burton burns his lamp and charts our passage; much talk, again, of how the rattling of pods, the chants, the singing to drumbeats will appease them; of how the crushed leaves, the ash, the scattering of shredded bark of stinkwood touched to a drip of blood from the loins of anyone willing to be pierced with a shard of cowrie shell will slow their progression— ("Just a scratch, John," Burton says, and he lets them make the laceration); much telling of how the taking of a bit of gore from any porter, guide, or bearer willing to be penetrated with the tip of our stolen calipers will keep them back—will keep the Paca Bunta (or, as those who say they have seen them say the name: Bunta, simply Bunta) back, and then again, there is much talk from the older ones who dig their sleeping hollows deeper, who have lost their share of surplus flesh in the district called the Land of Ants—that nothing will.

("Clean bone," says Mgongo Thembo when we ask about the drumbeats.

"Broken reed," he says. "Knife no blade. Slow bucket."

"Bad news, then?" I ask him.

"Hoo! Bad, sir," says Mgongo Thembo. "Hoo! Hoo! Very much bad.")

There are those among our party—mainly the guides for hire (one of whom, I suspect, has taken my pocket pedometer)—who say they have seen the great nests of the Paca Bunta in the grasslands—the mounds they build above their subterranean cities; the quarters for their excavators; barracks for marauders; chambers for egg cases; crypts they use to keep their stores of stolen shreds of meat.

There are some that travel with us—natives of the northern deserts—(one of whom, I now believe, has made off with my compass)—who say they have come across remains of men overtaken by the Bunta—carcasses of slave traders within the slack and rotting trousers, the corpses of their captives still shackled at the feet. This they speak of when they show us the blades they have fashioned from a shinbone or whittled from a rib. This they tell us when we ask if we are at all close to the cold stream Burton believes to be the source of the Wrong Way River or if we have passed the route of tusk trade that turns south at lower elevations; skirts—at some point—the mountain-high lake named Smoke in the Sky; approaches—in that proximity—the marshes made by the supposed seep of its headwaters, takes us farther into the interior, leads us overland, and in the end turns west out to the coast. This they answer when we ask if the centimeters of our map showing fields of scree and scoria we may assume to be reliable; if the concentrics of topography can at all be verified; if claims regarding the location of the lake that feeds the Wrong Way River we may take to be accurate; if rumors of the water we seek a dozen days west of where we are (or where we think we are, or where we were a week ago—a month ago—"some time ago" is what we say) have been borne out.

They answer with a lengthy bout of deliberation. They continue with a stint of bickering, proceed to hair pulling, foot stamping, howling and drum-talk, then finish with their fingers moving all across our map. Finally a bearer or a porter steps forward and points out to the horizon. He squints into the western light and says, "There the water lives, the sun waits; there the sky bends."

Burton smiles at such remarks, at what he takes as quaint. "The sky bends, John," he tells me. He claps the bearer on the shoulder. "Yes, yes! Good man," Burton says, and folds away our map.

He sits among them, nightly. He takes his notes into his tent, pencils in distances. He examines the specimens: seeds! Beetles! Leaves the men say are medicinal! He takes more interest in the tales the bearers tell of flying mice and diving spiders—expends more energy penning a recollection of a picturesque beggar, or in making a sketch of a spittlebug or chrysalis—than he does in taking a trophy tsessebe or a fine-horned buck. Evenings we see him, writing by the lantern light until he emerges through the canvas flap. He limps to the fireside, unwraps the bandage. He has Mgongo Thembo apply the masticated pods to the place where he has let himself be cut.

"Think of it, John," Burton says, "as a simple field experiment. Primitive medicine. Potential anti-infectives," and he sits with them in their circle, drinking the same fermented muck they drink, passing the bottle skin, poking the flames. I have seen the things that they will cook—bats snatched in their dangling sleep, mossed sloths, rodents that whistle; but nothing ant-ish, never a one of them kin-ish to Bunta. No, the things they devour they dig up or take from inside the carcass of a kill, pull from within the twist of sloughing innards, or pluck from contented sucking tight to a taproot: invertebrates defined, ash-dusted; writhing creatures they turn inside a foliage-fastened petiole tucked into leaf-tip and set among the coals to roast. Served hot. Never salted. Said to be tender. Stashed sometimes in their packs for a good long spell and retrieved for eating when advanced to what Burton likes to call "a fine putrefaction." They gobble, they slobber. They dress their beards with drippings and use an ankle as a napkin. Burton sits and shares such feats as these with them, while the steaks of a fine blue duiker I bring back from an evening's shooting go to waste.

"Phylum annelida," he says, blowing on bulge rolled within a steaming leaf. "Segmented, saprophytic. Similar to the common foetida." He licks at his fingers. "A species quite interesting for its protuberant sperm funnel," he says, "and the position of the slime tube, the concealed dorsal pore."

He holds up a hunk of something skewered. He sniffs the thing and says, "Come and sit, John. Eat."

("Fire stick," says the drum. "Black ash. Clay bird. Empty pot.")

They watch us eat—the Bunta do—Mgongo Thembo tells us. They send their scouts, he says, to learn our scent, to eat from the cast-off ribs of roasted kudu, the pieces of beast whose bones we have sucked and still bear the smell of our saliva, the dent of our teeth—parts we have so carelessly strewn about our evening fires. One gourd bearer whom I believe to be a half-wit (not withstanding his clever attempts to steal my pocket chronometer) says the Bunta lookouts sit upon the boughs of stinkwood we so prudently place outside our evening camp. There they wait until the morning when we empty our basins of whiskered shaving water and fold away our tents. And when we have packed up and moved on, they swarm in over the wet where we have pissed the last of last evening's embers out.

("Third moon," says the drums. "Sore foot. Stinkwood splinter. Yellow blood.")

It is said that the Bunta mount the body of a sleeping man in unison.

It is said that no amount of brushing or beating of one's body will dislodge a one of them; no amount of plucking will persuade their tiny biting parts to release their grip upon the flesh.

One tries to flee, not knowing that the attacking flank spans a full kilometer. One staggers, and falls—smiling—or so the bearers say.

"Hoo! Hoo! Very bad!" says Mgongo Thembo, elaborating.

"Ataxia," says Burton, "followed by euphoria. Undoubtedly a toxin secreted through the pincers. Formic in origin; paralytic, probably; initially sequestered deep in their salivaries."

"Rubbish," I tell him. "Daft talk and ravings. We speak of intruders at a picnic! Invaders of the pantry for a bit of damson jam."

("Bad hunt," say the drums. "Hornbill bird. Grilled root. Baobab.")

("Hoo," says Mgongo Thembo.")

"So few gourds left," I tell Burton when we move on in the morning.

"No shaving, John," he says. "No bathing. No side trips for hunting. No stops for tea."

We will drink—when we must drink—the watered blood and curdled milk in bottle skins the bearers keep.

We will break camp in the cool of early dark. Set off. Suck stones.

Leave before first light when the earth is still cool enough for their kin—for the kin of Bunta—to be stirring, to be unburrowing themselves; to be rolling away the balls of dung that seal their dens, to emerge from the sticky pistil of a night-blooming flower, to scuttle from the mouth of a fallen bird, creep from under the frond that made their midday shelter from the heat.

There is talk at night to these small things—these kin of Bunta—with links of undulating legs, chitin backs, and bivalved bodies. They speak to them—softly at night, to these arthropods that stretch the timbral membranes in their bellies drumhead tight to make their whirring songs or rake their rough-scored legs along their wings to speak. It is these small folk, who, our bearers say, will talk with Bunta. Will say our names to Bunta—the names of each of us—and tell them we have come far, that we mean no harm, that we want only to find the place the river was born in, to name the place the river was born in—*is* born in every day, they say—water, our bearers say, that comes the same as water before the birth of something they still are waiting for.

("High lake," says the drum. "Cold stones. Waterbird. Bright wing."

"A bit off course," I tell Burton of a detour through the hill country.

"Coleoptera," he says, of a beetle up his trouser leg.

"Coral bead," says the drum. "Ivory comb. Print cloth. Looking glass.")

These tiny beasts the bearers take with nets made of their hair, or with snares woven of vine, or with spider's silk procured by prodding large arachnids until strands are shot from ventral spinnerets (so strong is this substance, we have seen the great spiders here capture godwits and guinea fowl, wind them neck-to-tail with silk as if they were spindles, and to keep them from their frightful peeping—add a last bit about their beaks).

These kin of Bunta the bearers set loose from their nets, with great care unwind the strands of hair or vine or silk from what has been captured in the dark—untangle the needled stinger, the stylet, the beaded feeler; release the pedicle of mouthpart, proboscis, protuberant ovipositor. And then, snares undone, they kiss the iridescent shells of these arthropods never listed in our taxonomy, place them on their dark palms and breathe them off, set free to carry our message to the Bunta, back to their subterranean metropolis of tunnel and chamber.

"Tarawat!" they say to send the creatures crawling off or taking flight. "Tarawat!" they say. "Sik!"

("Low on salt," I tell Burton.

"Hypertrophy of foreleg," he says, of a hard-winged kin of Bunta.
"*Barton's Botany* is infested with book lice," I tell him.
"Sexual adaptation," he says, "for copulatory clutching."
"No more holcus-scones," I tell him.
"Highly effective," he says, "grasping through a wing slit."
"Sik," says the drum.)

"Say," I tell him, "we come to water. We find the stream—the one cold enough to be the outlet of the high lake we seek. Say we fill our gourds, our skins, and there we cross and follow."

"Yes, John," says Burton, puffing on the stick-pipe and passing it on. "Say we do."

"Would not all this talk of Bunta cease? Would the bearers say the Bunta stop and leave us at the banks?"

"Mgongo Thembo," Burton calls. "Ask the men, the drummers: If we find our way and we cross cold water—will it stop the Bunta?"

They begin the familiar rhythms. They scatter the stinkwood. Ash in the air, palms to drumskin: slap, slap, Bunta. Slap, slap, slap.

"Hoo! says Mgongo Thembo. "Bad, sir! Very bad! Tiny boats of folded leaf!"

(Slap, slap. Slap, slap, slap.)

"Tiny boats?" I ask Burton.

Burton smiles and shrugs. He rubs the wound inside his thigh and lets Mgongo Thembo apply the poultice. He takes another swallow. He is stupid with the drink. "Smoke, John?" he says, and he coughs and offers up the hollow stick.

I will not sit, as he does, at their fire. I will not, as he has, forego civility or relinquish the use of a napkin or plate. I will not crouch in the dirt and distribute our strands of trade beads, our shards of looking glass or our best bolt of calico to whoever comes calling at our camp—the hunting party, the slave escaping, the so-called local king who has for his kingdom castles of reed huts, scepters of chip-stone.

I will not sway with them to the sound of their chanting, or decorate my face with stripes of yellow clay.

Will not shed my trousers and dance about on one good leg with them in the firelight.

Will not lie down as he does upon the reed mat with the women the king offers us in our honor upon the night of our departure; will not bed them in the name of anthropological exploration; will not watch as they lift their bark skirts so I may select my favorite orifice; will not watch while they dress their heads with fat of kudu or smear their heathenish holes with an unguent of rancid butter.

I will not let the one who makes their medicinals feed me a leaf for the purpose of scientific inquiry; will not weave a fringe of feathers through my beard as a study in culture or let savages slather my genitals with mud.

"John," he calls, "come see"—that grin of his when he gets half mad!—and he shows me how big his prick has grown, how marvelously thick, and how the mud along the shaft cracks and flakes. And I see. And it has.

("Smoking stick," says the drum. "Yellow clay. Fine buttock. Coarse hair."

"Common sphinx moth—the order Lepidoptera," Burton says, when he stumbles to his tent and finds the shaggy creature lying dead inside the lantern glass.

"Low on gunpowder," I tell him. "Nearly out of lamp oil."

"Too badly singed," he says, "to be a proper specimen."

"Etching of dendrites on the lens of the telescope."

"Order of strepsiptera; vestigial forewings; life cycle notable for sexual dimorphism."

"Aneroid nonfunctional: atmospheric derangements."

"Rudimentary organs for mutual stimulation."

"Pocket watch crystal smashed; main spring over-wound."

"Penile maturation in periods of drought."

"Smoking spoor," says the drum.

"Swinging tail," says Mgongo.

"Calf of kudu," says the drum. "Blood on a stepstone. Torn flank. Old lion.")

I bring down a reedbuck. Heart wound. One shot. The bearers take their bone blades and slice the belly open. The porters set it roasting, dripping on a turnspit. The flesh is lean. We have no salt.

"This grassland variety, *Redunca arundinum*," Burton says, tearing at his portion. "Too bad it's nearly tough as mutton. Save the skin as specimen. Bottle up the blood."

The bearers drag in deadwood. Mgongo Thembo brings the last of our brandy. Burton swigs and soaks his beard. The bearers scatter the bark of stinkwood. The circle of sleeping hollows is dug. The hides are spread. Mgongo Thembo reports on the state of our provisions. Burton props his leg. I oil our pistols. The stinkwood crackles and smokes. The sun sets. The shapes of thorn trees and aloes grow dimmer. The boulders fade into the dunnish color this up-country landscape takes on at dusk. Silhouettes of acacias buckle in the updraft, limbs awash in the spark-spray of burning, in the dying lights above the dark-hilled horizon where the sun sleeps, where the water waits. Where the sky bends above the nameless place the river was born in.

Burton talks of women; I—of game, gun, and saber. He unbuttons his trousers. He shows me where his groin is dark and tender, how his prick is swollen hard. He takes a final swallow. He speaks of home—of the fields and the stables; of polished boots and the finest saddles. He slings his arm across my shoulder. The stinkwood snaps. The green sticks hiss. We sit side by side as the burning logs sink and shift, and we sit and we speak like men.

Night drums merge with the sounds in dreams—the chatter in the treetops; the hooting in the canopy; the snuff and root from the leaf-rot floor as a serpentine tongue is shot from a snout and comes back sticky with centipede or Bunta. Around us is the clicking of insect pincers in the stinkwood, their insistent drumming in the forest stands of ficus, the grind of a clock-key, of a hairspring winding.

They move along the limbs; they meet along a stalk. Exhibit organs for mutual inspection, rhythmic copulation, parthenogenic mount. Inseminating parts are spent and devoured. Stacks of eggs are inserted into stem slits, pumped into pith, deposited into corpses. Erect ovipositors are sunk into dung balls for leisurely incubation fueled by decay. Larvae hatch, crawl, sleep. Duplication of wings. Exoskeletons split. Emergence from the nymphal skin is marked by the beat in a drum-hollow belly, by a membrane of vibration or a rasp-edged appendage that signals their solitary, synchronized flight; the announcement of night navigation by moon, by stars, by flame; by hot sparks that the night wind lifts. By burning wick that illuminates our tents and brings a shadowy flit across the span of canvas: their jointed bodies, their symmetry of wing.

There are apparitions in sleep; there is sense in dreams: Burton, in the lamplight, standing at the tent flap, firm, unfevered. "John," is all he says, all I need to have him say. All I need to hear above the ratcheting of limbs, the tapping on the lantern glass. The night turns cool. The narrow cot. The taste of brandy on his tongue. Pulse of drums. Beard to chest. Crest of hip to crest of hip. Clutch of foreleg. Drip of loin. Limbs pressed, damp. Muscled cleft. Dungish hole. The skin stretched tight.

("Sik, sik," is the sound of the wingbeats on the canvas, the membrane in the body.

"Calabash," goes the drum. "Many seeds. No worm."

"Hard belly," comes the sound.

"River weed," says the drum. "Slipstone. Mud in the mouth.")

Morning, and two bearers are, as they say, among the missing—snuck off, apparently, sometime in the night; taking with them loose tea, our knife for skinning, Greenwich watch, match tin, saltcellar (empty), brass telescope.

"Stars, John," says Burton, "They haven't taken the stars and we still have the sextant." I see he will not stand without his crutch. He barely sets his weight upon his leg.

We are slowed down in this hard country. There is no tree, no shade nor stream. Thickets of heath adhere to the hillsides. Thornbush acacia sprout from the rock dust. Barrel-stemmed cacti with yellow spines live in the seams of basalt. The terrain is strewn with slabs of mineral: chert and obsidian, great fractured plates of it, mostly volcanic, now hot again clear through the boot. Burton struggles along with his crutch of stinkwood—off-balance as we travel the rough gullies. He calls to me when we must clamber over the rubble of rock and brush. He falls back when the trail we make tilts up.

We are made to take our rest out in the sun, but there is no sense in this.

We lighten the weight in the loads of the bearers: toss away a cook pot, a kettle, the trade beads, the cutlery.

The cactus has pulp. We suck the juices out.

Mgongo Thembo retrieves a spiny rind we toss off and shows us the single Bunta clinging to the wet.

"A large specimen, a good two centimeters," says Burton. "Banded cephalothorax, longer antennae—a lone scout, perhaps, or just a lost individual." He lifts it to eye level and speaks in a whisper: "Have you come to catch us, little fellow?"

"Hoo!" says Mgongo Thembo, smacking his head. "Very bad luck to speak to Bunta! Talk only with kin or cousin!"

"Very much pardon us!" he tells it, and sets the fruit skin away from us upon a rock. "Tarawat!" he says, bowing. "Sik!"

("Low on lump sugar," I tell Burton. "Out of iodine."

"Diperta," he answers, swatting at a sweat fly.

"No more rope. Short on pitch. Half spool of rush twine. Fish hooks rusted."

"Probably related to the lowland tsetse."

"Matches damp. Candles melted. Whetstone cracked. Spirit level leaking."

"Stone-fly species. Partial to sucking. Seminal vesicles packed into appendages."

"Vial of emetic left uncapped and empty. Nearly out of vitriol. Last dose of laudanum."

"Tiny soul," says the drum the bearer now is beating. "Low cloud. Great swarm. Long walk. Clotted water.")

We lean into the hillside, stepping slantwise, making a foothold in the spaces between stones. Mgongo Thembo, from somewhere in the lowlands, is unused to such climb and descent. ("Hoo!" he says, when we show him the map and we ask which of these dark countries he is from. "Hoo!" he says. "Far!") He slips from the trail and slides a ways into the rift. His pack splits. The strap breaks. We watch the flask of ink explode, the biscuits become airborne, the sextant bounce. My horn-handled knife is a small glint of blade stuck fast and far away between the rocks.

"Hoo," says Mgongo Thembo, when we haul him out. "Hoo."

("Sik, sik, sik" comes the sound of what we first think to be drums, but drumbeats could not reach us here across these corridors of rock. "Sik, sik, sik" it comes again—the beat and rattle of the kin of Bunta with bodies that blend with the color of the stones, wings the shape of blades, appendages of thorns.)

New terrain ahead of us: grass, baobab, grass—a broad stretch. Beyond that, a green border. "Wetlands," says Burton, "At last, perhaps, the river valley." He jams the sharp end of his stick in a crack. "John," he says, "Give a hand and help me up."

There is a dark place on his trousers that is stained with what leaks from him, and when he moves, there is a smell, however faint, like the kind from certain fungi. Sweet, yet fetid—the sort that might bring flies. I sniff at my clothes and wonder if the stink is just the decomposing cloth or the powdery earth mixed with my sweat and turned to slime. Or is it I, at last begun to rot?

"Hymenoptera," says Burton about something hovering. "Cousin to the ichneumon wasp."

The bearers hoist their packs. We walk on.

We pass though the flatland: high grass, hard earth, herds of gazelle known only by the nod of head and horn and black pellets of spoor.

The trail becomes thick, the terrain wet, without the growth of succulent or thorn. Here is all ficus, liana, broadleaf shrub. Bromeliad tucked in crotch and fork. There is seep, great rot, smells we are uncertain of. Overhead is heard the hush of larval forms chewing though bud tips—the leaf miners, the pith splitters, the soft-bodied creepers and cocoon spinners. We hear the rising stridulation of forms largely arboreal. The earth gives. We clutch vine and runner. Misjudge handhold, fooled by aerial root. We fall into the muck. We see light ahead where the foliage thins. Breakthrough of sun. We find the riverbank.

What water is this?—we ask our bearers, as fools would ask: could this be the source of the great Wrong Way River? And we unfurl our map, spread it flat with our forearms, and take our pencils up.

"Why," says a bearer, "this is the water that settles in the corners of the eyes when a thorn finds a home in the foot."

"What wets the skin," says the other, "when the sun is high and the man must be running."

"The same," says the last, "that fills earth holes in the season that the sky is dark."

"That water, sir," says Mgongo Thembo. "There is no other!" And so we lift our arms to let the paper loose and roll back up.

He brings us our box-kit of instruments, releases the brass catch, lifts the teak lid: survey compass missing its needle; condensation under the stopwatch crystal; elevation thermometer cracked clear through, leaking quicksilver onto the felt. But it is no matter—no use would there be in making our measurements; this river feels too warm to be source water. We know the instant we step in.

We shed our clothes, and bathe in the shallows. Burton soaks himself, squeezing fistfuls of sopping river grass into the spot where he was cut. "John," he says, "look here," and waves me over. "The swelling has subsided somewhat," he says. "Well? What do you think?"

I think, sometimes, I hear the drumbeats when we are too many days beyond the sound of any drum or village.

I think I hear them say the name of us, or any name I say along to the sound of them, or anything I seem to want to hear.

Some nights I hear them say the same sik, sik, sik they say to kin of Bunta.

In dreams, some nights, I know the kind of language that they speak.

We rinse water vessels of the soured curds, dark clots. We fill the skins. We fill the gourds. We find a trampled path to the water where hippos lumber along, gather momentum, fall upon their bellies and with great abandon and joyful bellow, mud-slide in. We watch the shores for what moves and what might slither. We see a great stork-beaked thing lifting its yellow legs, stalking the pools. I point and ask a bearer, "What is that?"

He puts aside the spearhead he is winding to a stick. He looks upstream. He speaks to Mgongo Thembo. They gesture long, jabber, put thumbs to their foreheads, waggle their fingers when it shakes its feathered crest. They find our other man, a porter, for consultation. They argue, deliberate. Commiserate with Mgongo Thembo.

"Well?" I say.

"Bird, sir," Mgongo Thembo says. "They say it is a bird. Hoo, very big, sir. Very bad luck to point at such a bird. Very much bad."

"A bird, John," Burton says, and he calls for his book, and

for his pen, but we have no ink. He takes up his pencil, but he makes no note or mark. "Marabou or white-bellied stork," he says. "Habits comparable to those of the vulture or other carrion eater."

"Comforting," I tell him.

"John," he says, "We'll walk out yet. The both of us have grown too thin to be anyone's meat."

We make camp, peg the tents, prepare to rest and study our maps. There is water here, at least. And game, good shooting: Gemsbok and water buffalo at the stream, come to drink. Evening brings an easy kill. We have only the bone blade to cut the skin and section the meat. We call the bearers, both of them, to clear a fireplace, but they sit and look away from us. Mgongo Thembo speaks with them, but still they sit; they will not come.

"Bad smell, sir," says Mgongo Thembo, pinching the end of his nose. "Blood in the wound stinking like a river sitting still; like a lake with no stream out."

"Sik, sik, sik," I hear the bearer tell the porter on his little skin drum, tapping out his song as the night sounds start.

"Tarawat, sik, sik," as they pile on the stinkwood.

"Sik, sik, sik"—becoming a comfort—the bearer's small brown fingers to the hard stretch of drumskin. His thumb across his thumb and his hands the shape he would make for a shadow play of butterfly or bird, bending at the wrist, fading to the distant backdrop of a dream. Becoming the recollection of a cry between our breaths, between the beat of beating hearts, between the dull and final pulse within swollen appendages.

"Sik, sik, sik"—it comes, calling back the morning with its slow smoking cinders and the rocks varnished black by the resin of the stinkwood.

"Sik, sik, sik"—through the circle of sleeping places where the porter and the bearer had pretended to sleep but had looked to the east where the sky is known to bend and the first light lives. Where they waited for the light and they abandoned the hollows they had scooped from the earth for the comfort, for the crest, for the slope of the hip.

"Sik, sik. Bird, sir. Bone blade. Horn blade."

"Sik, sik. Sucking bee. Honey gone. Rope over."

"Hoo, sir! Hot leaf. Folded boat. Bad, sir."

"Coleoptera. Hymenoptera. Dorsal pore. Damson jam. Formic in origin."

"Stinking river. Bad, sir. Sik! Sik! Sik!"—is the sound in the circle of snouts just out of sight of the circle of sleeping places; whiskers quivering to the scent of a fine putrefaction; to the smell of our stinkwood fire gone out, of his limb gone dead, of the dank and mildewed canvas we drape upon the poles of stinkwood to carry Burton out.

"John," Burton says as he settles into the litter, "I'm afraid I've become such a bother this trip." We set the poles upon our shoulders and we lift him. We step into the river. The stones are all slime, all humped—pushing hard into sole and instep by his weight. The cobbled bed gives way to the soft bottom and the river comes up waist-high, pouring in and filling up the sling to his neck.

"Odonata," Burton whispers, of a flat-winged fly that has landed on the canvas. "Rectal gills for respiration; larval forms are largely aquatic."

We push apart the tangled roots of hyacinth to make a path through the spiked blooms and stalks. Bottom silt rises around us. We are red-brown and rusted where the water leaves it mark; black upon the streamer of bandage that floats beside us—a foul decoration undone by the current with the slough of crust and skin and muscle. We drag the litter up. We cough and spit away what has slid inside our mouths. The hammock leaks its runnels down the slope.

"John," he says, and he has me by the wrist. He pulls me down to him, close to his mouth. "Tonight we will camp with open sky above us. We will see the stars and find out where we are. And when the drum sounds start and the fever makes me sleep, you will set the lantern close by and use the blade."

The bolt of calico is wet. I take the cloth in my teeth and tear it into strips.

We sit, the three of us, and watch the river. Clouded where the canopy breaks. Opaque where it skims over rock. Bright where it parts for a snake.

"Hoo. Snake, sir," says Mgongo Thembo.

We watch the sway of river grass, the downstream spread of silt. The spiked blooms of hyacinth we have broken loose.

"Hoo!" says Mgongo Thembo, now on his feet and peering upstream at what is coming: a flotilla of leaf fall, wide as the river is. A fleet of green, pushing through flotsam of petal and twig. Leaf after leaf is what is coming, turning in the current, creased along the midrib and keeled by petiole, brimful of tiny, antennaed passengers, riding pincer-tight.

"Hoo! Bad, sir!" says Mgongo Thembo. "Sik!" he cries as he is scrambling up the bank. Burton's mouth is open. We bind his wrists with rush twine so he will not dangle. We tie him at his feet so he will not thrash. The sun is higher. The clouds have parted. It is past the time for leaving. It is getting hot. We will be late today in starting up.

We will stay ahead of them, the Bunta. We will keep on now, now that we have crossed this river. We will keep a steady pace this time, making progress, leaving their battalions behind us. We will be moving now while they are bivouacked at noonday, while they are awaiting the return of the ones sent out to reconnoiter but return bearing no news of our direction, no notion of our whereabouts; telegraphing down their ranks with the tap of crooked antennae and the wagging dance of distance; moving onward as their marching narrows to the trickle of single file, flowing over what has fallen and withers on the floors of the rainy forests, winding through the stems of the grass on the great savannas, scrambling over rubble of clod and pebble, tumbling into the craters we have made where our boots have stepped and sunken in, deep with our weight.

We will be far beyond them—the Paca Bunta. Ahead of the procession that slows down but never stops for its stragglers, dilates with the convergence of their bodies, distends with the spreading edge of their numbers, the flux of a multitude that swells, surges, widens as the red-brown water of a river spills over where no river ever is.

Tonight we will camp and wait for sleep and the sound of drums from somewhere. ("Reed mat. Marabou. Blood melon. Cold river.")

We will listen between our cries; we will wait between wingbeats. ("Full basket. Palm heart. Pomegranate. Wasp honey.")

The pulse of the blood will come, and the sound of palms to the drumhead: the beginning hum and timbre of a skin stretched tight. ("Tusk. Tusk. Mud wallow. Baobab. Weaverbird.")

We will wait for the drums—what we hope will be drums—but we know we will be left waiting. We will listen for the sound but there will be only the drumming from within a hollow abdomen, the vibration of a belly part.

There will be the buzz of a tibial spur, of rasped appendage pulled along a cross-scored thorax.

There will come the sound of flint clean-flaked to a spearhead; the chip-sound of rock becoming a cutting tool, drawn across our limbs or a limb of stinkwood; the saw of a river stone turned into a blade, sent though hide, through skin, pushed through muscle; the sound of a rib whittled sharp for penetration, wound at one end with a rush-twine handle, slim and sharp for the piercing of the femur, fine-edged and serrated for the slicing of meat.

We will hear the noise we will make upon the body by the lifting lights of sparks and the flames of stinkwood: the sound of a sliver of chert, the sigh at the insertion of a shard.

The singing of obsidian, of basalt, though flesh.

The sound of bone on bone.

Ark

The daughter notes how the leaves droop, the way the stems bend and wilt: hollyhocks, hydrangea, blue meadow rue. The delphiniums are long gone. The roses: going. The horse chestnut has lost its leaves a season early. The square that once was lawn has long since turned to thatch.

The daughter hands her mother the hose. "Aim," she tells the mother. "Shoot for the roots." But there is little that the mother can do: wash a dish, wipe a counter, run the boy his evening bath but never let the water run. House rules now apply with the mother newly in the house: no sweets for the boy before dinner, no bad grammar, no taking out the car.

"This heat will kill me," says the mother with her finger on the trigger. "A person could be six feet under," she says. "At my age, a person could be dead."

Deep in the garage, the shovels are a jumble. The nuts are greased and dusted tight to bolts. The drill bits are brittle. The screws are jarred. The spade and the claw are clumped with last summer's mud. This year's husband is in there somewhere, sorting through the fishing gear and searching for a creel. The hedge clipper is crusted with cuttings. The pick-axe is flaking with rust. The daughter chips a hole in the rock-hard yard and drops the car keys in.

"I'm not a prisoner," says the mother. "Don't think for a minute I've got no place to go."

"Haven't," says the daughter. "And spare me the double negatives." She fixes her grip on the pick-axe handle, feels the heft of the weight. She approximates the height of the mother, establishes the arc of the swing and imagines where the point will hit. Predictions are grim. Restrictions temporarily lift: kiddy pools permitted even Mondays, sprinklers allowed odd Saturdays, hand held irrigation alternate Sundays. Sermons are heard. Praying for rain is routinely the topic. The preacher was seen sneaking a drink to peonies wilting in a window box. Warnings have been issued. Penalties are harsh. A summons was slipped in with the parish mail. Periodically the sky will darken. Sometimes the clouds will gather. Unfortunately, the ceiling always lifts. What sounded like a splat of rain was heard one morning early, but it was just the mailman spitting in the dust.

"Neither rain nor hail nor dew at night," says the mother.

"Too hot for hail," the daughter says, dragging the hose. She turns the faucet up for something between a gush and a trickle.

The burnt leaves crackle. The scorched grass shrivels. The soil seems to hiss. But the earth has made itself a rock and wards off the cure. "Spite," says the daughter, as the stream just puddles in the gutter. A panting sparrow swings on a withered petiole. A little river fills the street.

"It don't matter," says the mother. "Everything's dry as a dead dog's bone."

"Doesn't," says the daughter. "And, please," she says, "don't talk at all if you must talk like a hick."

Here comes the other daughter, sauntering up the drive. Older, she is—older than her sister and more dried up. She lives alone and motherless. Her heart is light because of it, though full of grit. "Do I smell rain?" she says, sniffing. "Or is that dust?"

"Ashes to ashes," says the mother. "Dead as a herring. Dead as a duck."

"If you ask me," says the older daughter, "we'll soon be out on street corners, begging for a drink."

"We should all be on our knees," says the mother.

"And praying for a deluge," says the younger daughter.

"Melting of the polar caps," says the older daughter. "Rising of the oceans. At this rate we'll be drinking up the sea."

"See?" says the mother.

"Get in the house," says the younger daughter.

"Make me," says the mother.

Inside the house, the ark is at the dock. The sea is crepe, furrowed and running a water-based blue, lightly salted where the boy has been sprinkling. Dishrag clouds have been clustered and hung. Paint has been applied in shades of gray. The dove and the sprig are poised. Noah is positioned beside the hatch, staff raised for keeping count. The boy is busy boarding animals two by two: bears, horses, monkeys, ducks. Flamingos, tigers, flying foxes are stepping up the ramp. "Lovely," says the mother, the grandmother to the boy, the mother of the daughters. "Except that there were no flamingos way back then."

"Use your imagination, Grandmama," says the boy.

"Don't sass," the mother says.

Down at the lake, the scum has started to stink. The rocks are baked, painted with algae. The ducks step hot-footed, too parched to quack. The fish are seared, bellies silvered. Fins surface in the smothering mud, circling and plowing the silt. On the dock sits this summer's husband, polishing lures and detangling the tackle. He is sleepy with the heat and recounting a recent bout of pillow talk. "Two weeks," said the younger daughter, the mother of the boy, estimating the duration: this resettling of the mother.

"Two weeks," she had said, setting down his favorite dish, in lieu of something fishy.

"Perhaps three," she had said, presenting something baked, by way of bait.

"A month or so, but nothing more," she had promised, "and how about some pie?"

But now the fruit is shriveled. The birds have pecked the peaches from the trees. The cherries are only their stones. The lakebed is rock. The bottom is cracked, slick with pools of mud, which—if one would step—would pull and clutch. The population of ducklings is recently diminished. The mother duck has begun a premature molt.

"It's too much, I tell you," says the younger daughter. "I'm pulling out my hair, at the end of my rope."

"You said you'd take her," says the older daughter, her mouth gone dry, but spitting some of her grit. "You said you'd keep her for a spell."

"A spell," the younger daughter says. "Seems like forty days and forty nights."

Nearby, something drums from a treetop: a dying locust, a dog-faced cicada, a woodpecker boring its final hole?

"Listen," says the older daughter. "That," she says. "I could swear that was thunder."

"A boat, and nothing but," says the younger daughter. "Oars on aluminum. Up the creek without a cloud in the sky."

The boat is beached. The husband is grim-faced and busy, sitting at the stern. He is greasing a reel. He is pinching a sinker.

The daughters are in the house supervising a sailing, the ark's departure. "A seer," says the older daughter, aunt to the boy. "A shaker, that old Noah," she says. "An expert at rocking the boat."

"Make him sit down," says the boy in his sailor's hat, painting on a whitecap and bolt from the blue. The older daughter sees the zebras, the family of elephants, trunk to tail, the troupe of possums toddling and pocketed; the bat, the wolf, the weasel; the terrapin tilting beneath a wave.

"Pathetic," says the older daughter. "Destruction of habitats, fire in the rain forest, drought right here in your own backyard."

"I could cut back on baths," says the boy, slipping a stingray overboard and sliding a skate into the crepe-hung sea.

The boy sets Mrs. Noah peeking though a porthole. "Cute," says the mother of the daughters, the grandmama, looking on. "Except it's much too hot in steerage for a poor old lady. A trip like that would do her in."

"Now there's a thought," says the younger daughter. "Deep-sixed, buried at sea."

The boy perches a flamingo upon the bow.

"Lovely," says the older daughter, aunt to the boy. "Except that soon there will be no flamingos left to flap around."

"Save it," says the boy.

Bedtime, and the younger daughter—the mother of the boy—is kneeling with an ear to the bedroom door. Inside sits the boy, spilling the milk, bathed and brushed for a dog-eared story.

"Tell me about the turtle, Grandmama," says the boy, still untucked and upright.

"Stuck in a bathtub," says the mother. "Landlocked. Lonely for its home."

"Did it get to its home, Grandmama?" says the boy.

"Hit by a truck on its way to the sea," she says, and smoothes the spread. "Flat as a pancake," she says, and she fluffs a pillow.

"Please!" calls the younger daughter through the keyhole. "Enough!" she says, knee-sore from trying to listen.

"And so," says the grandmamma, somewhat shouting now in the direction of the door, "they lived happily ever after."

"What's the moral of the story, Grandmamma?" says the boy.

"Shh," she says, tucking the covers. "Loose lips sink ships."

Out on the dock sits this season's husband. He is baiting the hook, dropping a line. "Darling," he has written on the note to be arriving soon, "Gone fishing. Don't wait up."

Out on the square that used to be lawn stand the two daughters of the mother—the older and the younger—looking at the sky. The sun is at a slant, starting to set. The boat is tilting on the rocks. The ducks roost tuck-billed on the beach. Just above the tree line, along the horizon, the light burns through the last of the leaves.

"Look," says the older daughter, the one withering. "Wasn't that lightning?"

"Sparks, most likely," says the younger daughter. "Could be cinders."

"But, listen," says the older daughter. "Wasn't that a rumble?"

"I doubt it," says the younger daughter. "More like a rattle."

"Done for," calls the mother, peeking from the upstairs window. "Curtains," she says.

The drapes are drawn. The window darkens. The smell of muck lifts from the lake-bottom. Here and there the puddles of black glint with the last of the sun.

Something that should be wetter slithers.

"Do I hear a rustle?" says the older daughter. "The leaves stirring?"

"More like hissing," says the younger daughter. "Snakes in the mud."

Something nearby flutters upward.

"I'd say that was a breeze," says the older daughter. "Wind, possibly. A change in the weather."

"Updraft," says the younger daughter. "Spontaneous combustion."

The older daughter puts her hand to her forehead—a brim against the fire of the setting sun. "But that," she says, looking past the circle of flame. "Over there," she says, seeing where the sky is sea-bottom black, all silt and billowing. "If you ask me, I'd say over there looks darker."

She points past the blaze to where the sky is churning with soot, merging with the dusk.

"If you ask me," she says, watching what is blowing, what is rising above the trees, "over there it's beginning to cloud up."

Seraphim

The bee has three natures. One is that she is never idle, and she is naughty with them that will not work, but casts them out and puts them away. Another is that, when she flies, she takes earth in her feet so that she may not be lightly raised too high in the air from the wind. The third is that she keeps clean and bright her wings.

—*On the Nature of the Bee*
Richard Rolle, Hermit of Hampole
1300 - 1349
Died during the first year of the Black Death in England

Augury of a sort in the kitchen; divinations behind the cupboard door: ciphers in a flour spill, swoons in the scullery, potatoes sprouting eyestalks gazing south.

"Portent, Prioress Clare," Sister Amanda tells me, tilting the dish, forking the whites into a froth. What eggs there are, the kitchen sisters are most afraid to crack.

Sister Issobel hears a humming in a dove's egg. Bette says it is singing.

Sister Meg tells me, "Clare, I believe there are bees inside the cloister wall."

Sister Marjorie brings an ear of corn from our garden, unsheathes the husk, strips the silk and shows me the tumorous kernels that sprout amid the pearly rows.

A stinkbug was caught on the quince bush; a book louse was discovered in a hymnal.

A dog tick was found on a Nubian goat.

"A herd of devils," says Sister Marjorie when she finds the cloven hoofprints in the patch of lavender.

"A flock of angels," says Sister Issobel when a pair of lacewing flies is captured in the nave.

"Omen," says Sister Marjorie, taking up her beads and tiny crucifix.

"Omelet," says Sister Amanda, sprinkling in the fennel, cutting in a sprig of leek.

A comet foretelling calamity, was spotted above the Isle of Man.

A star-nosed mole was seen hiding in the marigolds.

A whale was sighted in the bay.

By morning it lay stranded on the beach, leaking the sea between its teeth and bellowing; by evening, spouting blood from its blowhole.

The fishermen find their sails red-spattered. The villagers wake with their bedclothes smelling of salt.

"Fog," says the vicar. "Night fog and tide pressure; the disbursement of fish spray, leading to a seepage through keyhole and doorjamb."

"Excrement of honeybees," says the reeve. "Simply a migrating swarm, red with feeding on the nectar of roses; an off-course flutterment through town on a moonless night."

"No," says, our anchoress Sister Sigrid, when morning comes and she opens the door to her slop-closet. "No honeybees," she tells Sister Johanna, who comes to fetch away her bucket. "No wings," she says, "except the flame-bright ones of seraphim."

"It is not the crimson of a rose or tulip leaf," she says, receiving the bread that Sister Bette passes her under the slotted window of her cell.

"No," says Sister Sigrid, "it will not come by tainted air or sea. It will not be the red of a holly berry crushed by a beaky finch, or its barbed leaves that stain our hands and feet," she says, while Sister Bette waits for her to pass her back the empty platter.

"Only this," says Sister Sigrid, and she offers up her palm, shows the pierced spot. "It will be this," she says and Sister Bette sees the place in her where no nail was driven: "Here," she tells her, "His precious blood."

So Sister Bette tells me when she shows me where the rusty smear from Sister Sigrid's hand has dried upon the plate. No cause for concern, I tell her: we have, at times before, found our Sister Sigrid leaking.

We have, at times, found her singing in the old stone room wherein she stays, and swaying to what she says is music that the angels make. And there were times we found her thrashing on her straw-wove mat with her mouth so full of spittle and flecked with tongue-blood that she could not speak; her eyes turned up so hard for seeing heaven that we saw only the white.

And then, I must remind her, there was that day we peered into her darkened cell and looked about; how we held the lantern in at the end of the shepherd's crook to light the craggy walls, and found her hovering near the ceiling thatch and beam; how we begged her to come down, but she answered that the devil had made the earthen floor too hot for her foot.

Sister Marjorie says a hedgehog has dug himself a home inside the row of cabbage.

Sister Meg says the honeybees are humming off-key.

Sister Issobel spied a two-headed hop-toad hiding in the apples.

Sister Bette finds a double cherry with a single stone.

Sister Amanda finds a carrot in the shape of something she says holy women should not look upon and shows me a fig that sprouts what looks to be the vicar's nose.

Sister Salvinia tells me that the relic finger of Saint Agnes seems a bit more crooked.

No cause for alarm, is what I want to tell the sisters. No messages from heaven will be sent by comets or a falling stars.

No stock in what we hear by way of the friendly peddler hauling his cart into our yard, cranking his hurdy-gurdy and rattling his crockery. Bringing cinnamon, cardamom and yeast cake for the kitchen sisters; delivering cotton and flax for Sister Heart's spinning; toting packets of cochineal, bottles of indigo and cuttlefish ink; unwrapping from his bundle the pelt of a Chinese marmot from faraway Manchuria, a province so swarming with the creatures that they fall from cupboards and infect the citizenry by landing in the stew.

(Sister Amanda says the kitchen sisters now stand back to lift the larder latch and use the shepherd's crook.)

"Rumor," says the abbot in his letter, speaking of the news from Persia: subterranean thunder and hot blood from a mountaintop, igniting stones and sweeping the populace into the sea.

"Something seething," says the smith, "from the very same forge the devil stokes."

"Something boiling over," says Sister Amanda to the kitchen sisters, "from inside the pot he cooks up souls."

"Good morning, Prioress Clare," the bent-legged beggar tells me. "Something for the damned today?" he asks, soliciting a dinner at our kitchen door.

"Rumor, or the wrath of God, and that more mighty than the Devil's," the bishop writes in his reply. He trims the stiff-wing quill and dips the bevel in the ink. He tilts the taper to the crimson stick of sealing wax and spills the drops upon the folded page. He pushes in my thumb to make the print. "Hot," I tell him and he puts his hand to his lips.

"Forgive me, Clare," the bishop says, and cools my finger with his tongue.

The bishop says the vicar sees us; that the vicar watches when we are walking in the wood; that he knows we pray inside the copse of honeysuckle and kneel along a rail of wind-bent birch, an altar brightened by no candle but instead the moonlit blooms of bellflower and petals of the balm of Gilead.

The vicar sees us take the holy water of the brook.

He walks in when he pleases, any morning while Amanda and

the kitchen sisters are greasing the pans, folding fruit into the sweet roll dough. He comes unasked and asks the kitchen sisters to what hand I have in the cooking. They say he snoops about the shelves and asks to know the names of distillates I mix and bottle up; that he sniffs what roots and herbage hang and dry bunched stem-down from pantry beams, bound in twine that Sister Heart has spun; that he asks which ones are ones I like to call medicinal.

They say that the vicar wants to know: what manner of decoctions do I make the bishop drink?

The bishop says the vicar just likes to make his inquiries and is lacking in authority, He says that no one with a shred of any sense would listen to the vicar.

The bishop says his horse has thrown a shoe.

I hear the sound of one missing when he walks his horse upon the cloister stones—the clop and miss his stallion makes; the three-note tweet and whistling the bishop sings beneath my window when he holds him by the length of bridle strap; the song that might be just a lark's last summer madrigal, or notice from a nightingale who'd stayed up late.

I hear the saddle creak and the stallion snort as the bishop holds the stirrup still for me to mount, and then the crack down the paving stones when we escape.

I like the noise of hooves below us on the road, the splashing where the road is wet, and in the morning after he has ridden me home in time for morning prayers and Matins, the steady fade of hoofbeats down the rutted way.

I like to hear the bishop tell me that there is no sense in what the vicar says.

And certainly, no stock in what the peddler tells us. He brings us sea salt and tea. He shows us slips of roses from the crown of thorns cast off and sprouting where it once lay on that Golgotha hill—the roots of it still clinging to the clods of earth; soil from His Jerusalem, the peddler says, and dug up where His broken feet had touched. Taken from the very hills He walked.

"Every item authentic," says the peddler, bringing us a bottle of silvery flakes: scales of a fish, he says, that once swam in the Sea of Galilee—the one left over when the hungry crowd that came to hear was fed.

Bringing us what was left of the Last Supper: the unleavened crust and crumbs.

The peddler shows me fennel seed, garlic, fenugreek. He tells me he will sell the foreskin that the holy mother saved, or for a meaner price, the toenail of a lesser saint.

The villagers come to us on Sundays and ask to see the vial of sand soaked with the sacred relic of a martyr's blood; they ask to see again what once painted the lion's paw while saints prayed; what soaked into the arena floor, was scooped up and saved, and now will save us all.

The bishop brings me the notes he makes for Sunday sermon. He asks me what might he say anew about the shepherd's psalm, or about the recent crop of smutted wheat, or about the rain of ferrets that fell in Asia Minor.

And Sundays, when we share the Eucharist, we come before the bishop, and kneel along the rail. We hear him say the name of each of us as we take the sacrament of bread:

"Prioress Clare," the bishop says, and my mouth goes open, ready.

"Sister Amanda, Sister Issobel, and Sister Bette," he says, naming the kitchen sisters. "Take this, the bread of His body."

"Sister Marjorie, this is His body, sweet as a berry you bring from your garden."

"His body, Sister Cleopas—and may I inquire: are those feathers of an angel's wings stuck to your habit?"

"Our Sister Meg, who charms the bees, may this holy food protect you and spare you a stinging."

"For Sister Helen, here is the taste of His body, and do I detect your fresh lavender soap?"

"For Sister Johanna, here is the bread of His body and the strength you will need for the sick who need tending."

"Or dear Sister Decimina, eat of His body, and let us hope that's not piggery mud on your feet."

"For Sister Salvinia, who watches our flock, eat the bread of the Shepherd."

"For Sister Heart, who does our spinning, taste of the lamb and nourish your spirit."

"For you, Sister Pigeon, take the bread of His blessing and eat the heart of the dove."

And that is all of us, except the one of us who keeps herself inside the fieldstone cell. The bishop lifts the curtain where our anchoress Sister Sigrid is entombed and calls her forth. "His body, Sister Sigrid," says the bishop, as he puts the wafer where her tongue has bled from a recent fit. He asks her, as he always does, if she would say her prayers for him in holy solitude; asks her, as he likes to do, what needs she has that he may know.

"A bit more burr and thistle for my bed," says Sister Sigrid, and she backs herself once more into the gloom.

Sister Pigeon is first along the path to the darkened dovecote. She shows me where the doorway sags above our heads and I must bend to enter, unlike the way she flaps the wide folds of her sleeve and swoops herself inside.

I am unused to the murky air and the smell of nest and must. I am unused to the sounds of doves—their soft tremolo of prayer and hollow trill and the offerings of barbless feathers that float around us in the air.

Sister Pigeon catches each stray tuft. "Tiny gifts," she says, to teach us the patience that it takes to collect enough to fill a coverlet or await the flock she frees at the hopfield edge of forest, watches them lift away from sight, and later find them waiting for her on the cloister roof.

"Until the day," says Sister Sigrid, "when we shall see them swarm beneath the sun, and spiral on the stroke of wings into a cleft of clouds that takes them up."

Sister Pigeon says that some will set themselves afire flying into lightning storms, and some will just fold their wings and plummet straight into the claws of falcons.

She tells me that she stands along the greenwood edge and waits open-mouthed to catch what drips from the falcons' taloned feet, what percolates from Heaven and the hearts of doves.

"Hearsay," says the yeoman, when I catch him hunting in our fields, his hawk perched unhooded on his fist, the straps of the jess loose and dangling. "Mistaken," he tells me, when I say his peregrines and merlins are to blame for our missing doves.

"Falsehood," says the miller, to the charge his grain is tainted with a smut, that it makes them dizzy in their flight.

Sister Pigeon shakes the birdlime from her veil. She cracks loose the tiny coils of gray and white, and she leads me out.

"Deception," says the vicar of the story of an incident in the abbey dorter: the figure of an angel, carved into the balustrade, tore loose from its moldings and left by the belfry.

"Untrue," says the bailiff, of the siege in the Crimea, where troops of Tartars wait outside the fortress walls, load their dead upon the catapults, and daily fly the corpses above the city gates.

"Unwitnessed," says the sheriff, upon hearing of a crucifix nailed to a chapel wall somewhere in Burgundy—the crown of the thorns sprouted blood-red berries; the wound in His side dripped water from the sea.

"Unverifiable," says the reeve; that south of here are hoards of rats that strip bare the planted plots and gardens; that in the fields the stalks of wheat have withered; that the women sell themselves for bread; that in Sardinia they must eat their children and the dung of doves.

"Famine," the vicar says, "is what the Devil sends to test our faith. God fearing folk have nothing they should fear."

There are pumpkins in the cellar. Turnips. Potatoes. Apples in straw. Pears safe-laid in the dust of the blade saw.

There are bulbs of garlic braided by their top stalks; a plait of shallots hanging on a peg.

There are wheels of Stilton sitting in the springhouse, sealed in beeswax; there are goat-milk cakes lightly rolled in ashes, and some Sister Salvinia keeps wrapped in chestnut leaves.

Soft curds in a lidded crock.

Leek stalks. Dried limas. Barley. Lentils.

A barrel of hen-grain; millet for the doves.

Cobbed corn in the storeroom.

Gherkins in mustard.

Cabbage curing in an ironstone pot.

Sydre, pirry.

Burgundy—a quarter pipe.

A half jar of honey harboring the body of a long-drowned bee.

Hen eggs, pickled; red ones in beet juice; white ones in vinegar; dove eggs steeped in tea and studded with clove-seed.

There is a keg of mead and a quarter keg of metheglin.

There is a basket of raisins and a basket of walnuts.

Hard-salted herring, strung though the gill holes, curling at their tail fins.

Sprigs of basil, lovage, and tarragon wound at their stems with Sister Heart's twine.

Sister Amanda marks the months the pears need turning.

Sister Marjorie says the pumpkins should be wiped of mold all through the winter.

Sister Pigeon says the doves like fleece for nesting.

Sister Cleopas wants the rat holes in the henhouse sealed with shards of crockery.

Sister Meg says to smoke the bees before they swarm.

Sister Johanna says to feed those who fall ill with wine whey and caudle.

Sister Helen says to use her lye soap to wash the sick who soil their bodies.

Sister Meg says a boil will draw with hot beeswax and henbane.

Sister Salvinia says to bleed her when the veins of the Stilton are their bluest.

Sister Ruth says anyone too fevered to swallow solids should be fed a bread-and-butter soup.

("Lies," says the vicar, that a mob of hungry cottars pulled the landlord from his unfortunate palfrey and ate the beast on the spot.)

Sister Decimina says the brindled sow likes to snuff under her habit for the acorns she keeps hidden.

Sister Marjorie notches where we must prune the canes of gooseberry on the day that Heaven takes her and she cannot do it.

Sister Cleopas says the hens prefer a feed of apple-mash, cornmeal, and millet.

Sister Heart shakes the grain dust from the empty sacks; she cuts the armholes, turns the seam down for a collar and counts hem stitches.

Sister Johanna sets the fire in the scullery stove. Sister Amanda puts the big pot on and salts the water. Sister Helen takes her stick and pushes the grain sacks under. Sister Marjorie sprinkles in the mordant. Sister Amanda pours in the blood of cuttlefish and says the dye-water bath for a batch of shrouds must be three shades past black.

("Impossible," says the vicar, that a flock of rats fifty hectares wide murdered the swans in a millpond at Lincolnshire and then drank it dry down to the mud.)

("Improbable," says the bailiff, to tales of pestilence among the monks of Bestwick Abbey: buboes on the limbs, tongues swollen up; fever that heats the waters of the body and turns the blood into a sludge of pus.)

Sister Marjorie takes me to the garden, shows me what is becoming of our corn: the shriveled silk, the kernels grown to the size of dove eggs, but each a pustule leaking milky sap.

Sister Marjorie has turned her ankle in the hedghog's burrow.

Sister Cleopas thinks a fox has found a way into the henhouse.

Sister Decimina says the he-goat has taken to butting.

Sister Helen says her bar of laundry soap is as slippery as a puddle frog.

Sister Amanda spied a trail of sugar ants heading for the marmalade.

Sister Sigrid says that the spider that lives on a ceiling beam suspends itself on a silvery thread and speaks to her nightly just above her nose.

Sister Pigeon tells me she sends up her doves on a tether of moonbeams.

Sister Meg had a honeybee fly inside her habit.

Sister Johanna says her leeches are in need of a feeding.

Sister Salvinia reports the sow rolled in her sleep and smothered a shoat.

Sister Heart says that the black lamb's fleece is full of thorns.

Sister Issobel says the two-headed hop-toad hiding in the apples has grown as fat as a quince fruit and that it squirts Sister Bette with blood from holes in his nose.

"A familiar," says the vicar, who comes round the scullery door. "A pet that unholy women keep to do the Devil's bidding," he says, sniffing tarts and sweet rolls and looking for a sinner.

"Pray, sir, no need to stand outside the door the way a peddler would," Sister Amanda says. "Do step in and eat a proper piece."

We hold our mouths ready for the holy bread to enter. We watch the bishop step to each along the altar rail. We see the candle flame beside the crucifix, the hammered feet. We hear him name each one of us all in his salutations and we watch him make the sign across our faces. We see how the chasuble hangs from his shoulders. How the alb billows all around him as he retreats. I know how it hides the bones he is showing, and where the belt strap on his britches notches two holes past the place he used to buckle.

On Sundays, when the bishop comes for supper with us, he does not serve himself but hands along the platter of fish and tastes only his bread.

On Mondays, when Sister Amanda brings him his supper basket, she sees the bishop put aside his portion for the bent-legged beggar.

"More than enough," the bishop says, and slaps where his belly is when she asks if he feels fed. "We must save what we can if the wheat will be blighted," he says, "and keep it safe for folk in need of a full stomach to keep a greater faith."

Here is what I feed the bishop in the wood, what I find to fill him up: stems of sorrel and stalks of wild mustard; water in a folded leaf.

I see his sharp collarbones when the vestment is opened.

I feel the well of his pelvis when I slide into the dip of his belly, settle in the depths of his coarse hair. The stems of wheat may wither, is what the bishop says, but I still make his hard stalk sprout.

Sister Amanda says there is butter in the springhouse.

Sister Cleopas says we have a dozen hens still laying: eight young Dorkings, four North Hamshires.

Sister Marjorie says the bees are in the garden on the late summer heather.

Sister Meg says that soon there will be stores of honey in the skep.

"Nonsense," says the reeve, that the hollows of the body grow eggs that swell to bursting and spill a pus that flows like a honeycomb cut.

"Fact," says the manor clerk, regarding the method for confirming contagion: a dove held close to the mouth of any person carrying pestilence will expire by the vapors of contagion expelled.

"Fallacy," says the steward, that smew and sausage sold in the market stalls is maggoty.

"A fiction," says the vicar, that the last breath of the dying is smoke-black and that the heat of the fever is so great it cooks the flesh.

"Misinformed," says the steward when the kitchen sisters charge that the shops sell as swan and call it sea-fowl.

"Gossip," says the vicar, to rumors that a midwife in Newcomb fed her starving children a newborn's caul.

Sister Pigeon says we will eat the sparrows that the gray shrike skewers on the barbs of briars; we will tame the harrier and jess the merlin; we will eat the rats we pluck from the claws of dying hawks.

Sister Salvinia says we will go where the bellwether ram leads us. We will graze with the goats and the lambs.

Sister Amanda says the kitchen sisters will make a roux of butter and the bodies of weevils.

Sister Issobel says she will live on crumbs she licks from between Bette's lips.

Sister Salvinia says there is flesh enough to feed us on Saint Anne's relic finger.

Sister Johanna says the kitchen sister will find a way to stew the leeches.

Sister Marjorie says she will crack the stones of cherries between her teeth.

Sister Helen says there is nourishment in the washwater, sustenance in the tallow soap.

Sister Johanna says there is goodness in the stuff the sick spit up.

Sister Meg says we will don our veils of gauze and seize the skep before the end of summer; we will eat the beebread; we will chew the honeycomb.

Sister Marjorie says when the berry-stems are bare, there is always goat's-rue and gillyflower.

Sister Decimina says we will root with our noses in the dirt of the piggery; we will snuff about for acorns like the brindled sow.

Sister Heart says there is wool, there is hoof. There is milk, there is horn.

We wake for lauds.

We clasp our hands beneath our chins, say our prayers, take our places.

We lift our chairs so we will not scrape.

I stand one stair above the trestle table, above the bowed heads and the murmured prayer of each.

We thank Him for what comes from our garden, and for the milk from the goats; for the work of the bee, for the wool from the lamb.

The sisters hand around the strawberry Sister Marjorie has picked for us this morning: fist-sized, tonsured with a fringe of leaf, the skin of it roughened by the seed.

"So very like the heart," says Sister Amanda, "our Savior plucked from His chest and bid the twelve He chose to come and take it."

"So all would be saved, partaking of a piece," says Sister Cleopas.

"In all its sweetness," says Sister Meg.

"In all His joy," says Sister Bette.

"In all His sorrow," says Sister Issobel, "for the burden that it was, heavy as the fruit that bends the stem."

The kitchen sisters set the meal upon the trestle table: milk from the goat, millet porridge mixed with honey, cheese and cabbage, cornmeal cake.

I tilt the lectern. "Lectio Divinia." I find the place and lay the page open:

Behold, a sower; and the seed he flung from his hand took flight on the wind, and scattered.

"Like the dove flock when a storm cloud breaks," says Sister Pigeon, lifting the pitcher.

And some seed fell by the wayside and was taken by the birds.

"Like the sparrows in the hen yard that steal the millet," says Sister Cleopas, slicing off some corn cake.

And some seed fell on the stone, and sprouted, but withered when the sun was hot.

"Like the pepper-cress at the end of summer when the stream dries up," says Marjorie with a mouthful of porridge.

But some seed fell where the earth was good, and made its roots deep, and grew there by his word in the places we keep hidden where our hearts are fertile.

"On the south-hill slope, where the billy goats rut and drop their dung," says Sister Salvinia, passing the bread.

Together, Sister Issobel and Sister Bette tell her, "Hush."

Sister Johanna gathers up the rags we use to wipe our mouths. Sister Heart stacks the plates. Sister Marjorie saves the cabbage for the garden. Sister Decimina keeps the scraps for the piggery.

Sister Pigeon sits underneath the table. "Crumbs for the doves," she calls, "and nothing gone to waste."

Sister Salvinia grunts and stirs her cup.

The night bell rings with sunset coming. I can see the south slope hill from the vestry window; the hopfield and meadow and the trees that line the river; the river bridge and garden; the goat shed; the hen roost. Past these: the beach and bay, and beyond the pale road into the wood.

Below in the garden, is Sister Marjorie with her basket for the last of the gooseberries.

Sister Helen is reaching for the sacking where we hang the rope for laundry.

Sister Decimina is spilling acorns from the bucket to the pig trough, mud-spattering her skirts.

Sister Salvinia is smacking a goat's rump with her switch of willow. Calling in the last ewe. Lifting over the lamb. Shutting the gate.

Sister Johanna is shaking sheets from the infirmary window, a sachet of fleabane pinned to each.

Early crickets.
Sister Pigeon is cooing.
Sister Sigrid is singing from inside her home of fieldstone.
Sister Marjorie is chopping at the axe-stump.
The kitchen sisters are loud at their scouring.
I hear the hum of Sister Heart's distaff and spindle.
The second bell sounds to begin our silence.
All is quiet from Sister Sigrid's fieldstone cell.

We step the spiral of the night stair up to our beds, sheltering our candlesticks, climbing past the unsilled windows. We are climbing past a glimpse of field, a curve of stone, a square of hills. We are turning past the darkened bend of wall, a stone framed sky, a slot of stars.

We are told to shut our windows.

We are told to close the shutters to the night wind and moon-climb.

We have heard that there are vapors in the tail of a comet, in new moonbeams, and from well bottoms. In churchyard mists and peat-bog mire. In the secret burrows of star-nosed moles.

On trade winds, in sea air. In emanations from the fenlands and exhalations of the ponds.

"Untrue," says the vicar, hearing news of a derelict vessel adrift off the coast; tainted spices in the hull; dead sailors at the helm.

"Falsity," says the sheriff, hearing word that botflies settle on shipboard corpses and buzz to the coast and to spread the pestilence.

"Fibs," says the manor clerk, of forecasts based upon salt-spray calculations and prognostications made by sea-wind direction, that come this autumn season, death will reach us from southerly climes.

"Fabrication," says the reeve, of reports from afar: the Rhine going sour from the rot of the dead stuffed tightly into wine casks and sent down-river with the weep of their bodies leaking though the staves.

"Fact and corroboration," says the vicar, of news that nuns at Bowick made a pact with the Devil and thus infected the community of priests.

Pale light of moonset.

Cicadas.

Commotion in the henhouse: squawk and bark.

Pale road through the wood.

I sit beside the upstairs window. I keep the curtain cloth tied back, the candle lit, and my wimple on the table.

Night wind. Flame shift.

I listen for his whistle. For the hoof clap on the bridge boards. Bridle-chain jingle. Snort. Neigh. Rein-snap.

Some nights Sister Amanda knocks to wake me. Sister Johanna says my name through the door crack. Sister Cleopas, however, enters without my answer. Sister Pigeon tugs at my sleeve or taps me at the shoulder. Sister Salvinia prods me with the thick end of her willow-switch. Sister Heart brings me the shawl she made of her spinning. Sister Amanda brings a loaf. Sister Meg brings the mead flask. Sister Marjorie spits to her finger and tamps out my candle. Sister Issobel and Sister Bette stand at my window and wave to the bishop.

He leans forward in the saddle and he holds the stirrup steady. The roan steps forward. I swing over. My bishop lifts me up.

We lie in the wood. We make ourselves a bed. We make a cushion in the myrtle, a coverlet in green fern, our pillow in the coils of bittersweet.

I bring him nectar from the blooms of ragged robin, raspberries from the briars, cress from the brook.

I mash wild mulberry to his lips. He keeps them shut.

I push in the bits of fruit and seed with my little finger. He takes the berry from me and smears my face.

I take the water in my mouth, put my lips to his; he smiles, yet he defies me. He will not open. He turns away. He says that he thrives on nettles, charity, and pea shells; that he needs no wine or fruit, no mead.

He says that faith is his sustenance from Heaven, but on this earth, I am all he needs and that I am sweeter than the hard-stoned cherry, or the sweet snap-pea.

Shall I answer that the dead, despite their faith, find no sort of heaven in the end? Shall I say that they find only sleep among the stones and that that they drink what rain filters through their fleshless jaws, what mud trickles though the sockets that hold their wobbly teeth?

Sister Sigrid passes back her plate still full of bread, the wedge of cheddar left uneaten. She says the sacred wafer must be enough to stay us; His blood we sip will slake our thirst.

"Lies," says the vicar, that dying men are made to drink their blood, so fierce their coughing is, it breaks the vessels of the chest.

"Exaggeration," says the bailiff of the outbreak in the lowlands, where the barns stand burning, where wine cellars are left open, where livestock wander without herdsmen through the towns and she-goats and cows cry out for their milking.

"Precautions," says the sheriff of the district, who posts the latest warning:

Drink no milk of pigs or that of cattle with pustuled teats.

Crack no eggs from which you hear a peeping.

Carry a smelling apple or an orb of amber in your pocket.

Carry the foot of a coney or a tortoise for luck.

Chew rhubarb before breakfast. Eat feverwort at noon. Take a dram of henbane tea before retiring to bed.

Avoid night air. Avoid the evening breezes.

Avoid wind from caverns, smells from dung heaps, fumes from ditches. Shun holes dug for heaps of refuse.

Avoid a whiff of the breath of the dying.

Wrap your face with gauze when attending the afflicted.

Sprinkle sea salt on the floors of your bedchamber; wipe down the scullery with lemon juice and vinegar.

Catch fleas in the bed-sack with a double length of string dipped twice in honey; use cotton or twine; hang over the bedpost.

Fumigate linens with a powder of arsenic; bedclothes with talc, antimony, birdlime. Sprigs of lavender will mask any odor.

Expel no seed into dying women, and especially those with reputations of promiscuity.

Make a poultice of the rose-mallow that grows in the marshes; apply thickly to boils erupting from both armpit and groin.

When it is needed, evoke the names of the Holy Trinity.

When it becomes necessary, pray at the seventh station.

When it becomes obvious, fast and sacrifice. Seek absolution.

When all else fails, pray for intervention. Request a visitation. Request a dispensation from the apostolic see.

When it becomes evident, apply the rule of penance.

When it becomes evident, apply a soothing ointment: honey, lime juice, the rendered fat of strangled children.

When it becomes apparent.

When it becomes obvious, clear, plain.

Hereby posted by the district sheriff. The vicar is in agreement; the bailiff concurs. This, the second day of December, this year of our Lord: thirteen hundred forty-eight.

Sister Decimina is in the pigsty, bargaining with the peddler. He asks if the mistress of the pigs would like to trade with an honest peddler? Would she trade a sow's farrow for a magical fumigation? Burning in a watch fire, it purifies the atmosphere. Smoldering in a censer, it can easily be inhaled by an entire congregation. The odor will be pleasant, not unlike pine leaves in the forest; not unlike fern or lavender crushed underfoot; not unlike the smell of salt on the sea air.

Sprinkled on your pillow, bed lice will not enter your ear or nostril.

Sprinkled into a pocketful of posy, itch mites will not invade your person.

Sprinkled on the hen feed, your birds will not get spindleneck.

Smoked around the skep, your bees will leave in an orderly fashion.

Mix with ash and seawater and pour along a footpath. Cats, dogs, and flea-infected creatures will turn a wide berth away from you.

Scatter along your windowsill or blow into the baby's crib.

Strew along the groaning-board for good health and appetite.

Drop into the mouths of shut-ins groaning in their beds.

Sprinkle along a coffin rim, sprinkle on a pillow.

Place a pinch in the palms of the departed. Inevitable putrefaction will be greatly halted. Decomposition will be slowed down to a veritable snail's pace.

Mud-slugs, whip-worms, and soil-dwelling vermin will not enter in.

Sister Bette and Sister Issobel are at the scullery window, bargaining with the peddler. He inquires if the lovely kitchen sisters would want to see the wares of a peddler? Would they trade a gooseberry pie for his short-handled knife blade? Perfect for slicing. Best results when honed weekly. Ideal for kitchen chores and simple surgeries. Indispensable for shucking tumorous seed corn. For excising the unburst kernel, nicking the blister. Easy to handle when opening a vein. Handy for draining boils that erupt on the weak and fevered or for paring down a finger if you can't remove a ring.

Sister Cleopas is in the hen yard, bargaining with the peddler. He asks if the mistress of the chickens need the services of a peddler? He would trade arsenic or sea salt or dogbane for hen's eggs. Has she any cluckers molting? Any hens gone eggbound? He would trade for just the feathers. He could use a bag of feathers. Has she seen the rats rolling stolen eggs out from the nest box? Has she heard the hatchlings peeping as they are dragged away? Has she ever heard a tune played on his fine hurdy-gurdy? Would she like to have a listen? Would she like a try at turning the crank?

Sister Heart is in the doorway, bargaining with the peddler. Would the sweet spinning sister sell her yarn to the peddler? He would take her weaving; he would trade her tapestry. Well-spun wool is always profitable. Gauze woven for the beekeep has become quite marketable. Human hair is always in demand. Might he inquire: Is her hair quite long beneath her headpiece? Would she show a lovely hank of it? Would it reach below her breasts?

Sister Johanna is at the infirmary window, bargaining with the peddler. Would the blessed healing sister share her medicinals with a peddler? He would gladly buy her tinctures and her herbal preparations. Healing draughts and potions have become very popular. Poultices and ointments are all in short supply. Has she had much luck with spiderwort? Has she made a cure with garlic clove? Has she found that a fever breaks when chewing tinkerweed? Has she noted any effects of a strong horsemint tea?

Sister Meg is at the skep, thumping one for honey. She is listening for a buzz. She is bargaining with the peddler. Could she spare a little honey to sweeten up a peddler? Is she at all familiar with the protective effect of bee-sting venom? He'd be happy to determine if a bee's gone up her skirt.

Sister Decimina is in the pigsty, bargaining with the peddler. The mistress of the pigs will not trade the farrow hog. She will not give up the brindled sow. The peddlar says he would trade a tin of pig-teat balm for a sniff of her wimple. Good for maintaining tail curl. Helpful for treating snout rot.

Sister Pigeon is near the cloister roof, halfway up the ladder. She is cooing down a pair of doves; she is bargaining with the peddler. He asks if the gentle Sister Pigeon could show some kindness to a peddler? He would offer up for trade a recently procured relic: a feather from the wing of the archangel Gabriel, retrieved from a distant cloudbank and undoubtedly lost during last summer's molt.

She might like to make an offer. She might like to reconsider. He would gladly hold the ladder while she's mulling it over. He would take a pair of her loving doves if she could use a perching peg. Might he see the gray one's tail feathers? Might he help her hold the ladder? He would trade a bar of cuttlebone if he might hold her ankle.

Sister Sigrid is in her anchorage cell, praying for the peddler.

Sister Salvinia is at the goat-yard gate, bargaining with the peddler. He asks if the keeper of the goatherd would spare a word with a simple peddler? "Such an old goat I am," he says.

She replies, "Not so very."

He asks if she would need a jar of nanny wax? Would she need a set of clippers? Could she use a dandy whipstick instead of that willow rod to chase the goat-flock through the gate?

Does the he-goat mount the she-goat?

Is it true that the Nubian breed is the most intractable? Would she like to hold the whipstick? The finest braided leather, stiff at the handle. Stinging yet supple. He may possibly have a sample among his stock of merchandise. She could try out a new one. A free demonstration: he could show her his haunches and she could give him a whack.

Sister Helen is at the laundry tub, bargaining with the peddler. She is wringing out clean wimple-cloths, tipping out the rinse water. He says he'd swap for a cake of that yellow soap she uses. He could use someone to scrub his unreachable areas. He could use a good soak in a tub that big.

Sister Marjorie is at the cellar door, bargaining with the peddler. She is sorting out pears with soft spots and salting the cabbage. She is waxing the cheddar; she is polishing a pumpkin. The peddler asks her if she could spare a sip of that mead she is stirring. Does she plan to spill the dregs from that bottle of wine? He says that the cellar is so dark, may I offer you a candlestick? So cool it must be, may I come in from the heat?

Sister Decimina is in the pigsty laughing with the peddler.

Sister Sigrid in her enclosure, praying for the peddler.

Sister Salvinia in the fen, bagging leeches.

Sister Decimina in the pigsty bargaining with the peddler.

Sister Decimina in the pigsty with the peddler.

"*Preposterous*," writes the abbot in his letter to the bishop and denies all rumors that his monks are unwell.

The bishop unfolds the abbot's letter and has me read:

Dear bishop,

Preposterous that one would think the monks have fallen ill. Put any doubts you have to rest, for we are well at this writing, but appreciate the inquiry. We are very well indeed, and well about our prayers and work.

By the way, dear bishop, how are all at the priory? Have you noted any persons complaining of dyspepsia?

Brother Rupert is hard at work in our scriptorium, and extends his salutations. He is in receipt of the manuscripts. He is undertaking restorations. Currently illuminating Ezekiel and emblazoning Ecclesiastes.

Have you noted any person spewing blood or brackish vomitus?

Our weather has been warmer than one might have expected. But the nights remain cool, and the air is most pleasant. Has your weather there been dreary? Are the wheat fields quite dry?

Have you noted any evidence of changes in the climate?

Have you had much rain?

Any hailstorm of clots? Perhaps a downpour of crimson?

There have been absurd reports of celestial phenomena—specifically, a crucifix of wood and gilt was sighted over Burgundy.

Have you noted any person blotched about the face with a wine-hued stain?

The frequent rains we have been having take their toll on the local thoroughfares.

Have you noticed any persons slumped by their scythe and sickle?

Passed anyone at all lying prostrate in the ditches?

We have had a lovely wedding for sheriff's only daughter. I was asked to officiate. It was attended by many. The bride wore the heirloom gown saved by her recently deceased mother. The nave was a bit overdone in elaborate decorations: garlands of lily of the valley and spumes of white posies. Here and there were bunches of garlic cloves. The groom is a distant cousin to the alderman. I believe he is in ownership of considerable acreage to the south.

Do I correctly recall, good bishop, that your churchyard is quite sizable?

On your next visit to the priory, please send my blessing to the sisters.

Prioress Clare, no doubt, has been kept well occupied in her duties; please my fondest regards.

And regards, as well, to Sister Amanda and both the kitchen sisters; many a morning I find myself longing for their cherry buns.

Might you ask Sister Johanna if she's had success with leeches?

Has she tried their application on apostumes near to rupture?

Have you noted any persons who must hold their arms akimbo?

Have you noted any swelling in the hollows beneath your arm sockets?

Have you lately assessed your privy parts for the development of pus-tumor?

Please ask Sister Johanna if she will have room to spare in her infirmary, or does she still shelter cripples, scab-heads, and lepers?

Have you space in your churchyard should ours fill up?

Brother Henry's dementia has much worsened since your visit. He is nearly bedridden and afflicted with toad-warts. I, for one, am distressed by unusual headaches. Attacks of peevishness. Occasional night sweats.

Have you awakened any morning to find you have been visited by a succubus? Your seed pooled on the sheets? Your privy-limb sore?

If Sister Helen can spare several cakes of her lavender soap, we would most welcome a parcel. I recall how the sheets were scented when I was a guest of the priory.

Does Sister Decimina still smell like a hoggery?

In closing, I remain Alfred, Abbott of Dorset, and send this to you in the name of the one who gave Himself to save us, to be our salvation, and to make the word flesh.

This, the first day of January, in this year of our Lord: thirteen hundred forty-nine.

The bishop folds away the page. The flask of mead is empty. The ferns that made our bed are broken. We find the bread the kitchen sisters baked; we spread the shawl and make a leaf our plate.

Beyond the trees, beyond the fields and the road, and far past the priory gate, the steeple bell rings out for Prime. A chaffinch starts its peeping on a branch above us. The glowflies are gone. The night crawlers retreat. Runnels of the sun break the boughs and leaf-thatch. Far off, our rooster sounds the coming of the light.

With the dawn upon us, Sister Cleopas would be in the coop now, nudging a hen, handing out an egg.

Sister Bette would be in the kitchen now, filling the sifter, dusting the board.

Sister Heart would be kneeling on the wool of the lamb, her lips to her crucifix before she starts her spinning.

We ask a blessing for the coming day. We thank Him for the bread upon our plate. We pray this will not be the final meal we eat.

I do not ask the bishop how it is that he believes; how he knows that he is Heaven bound; how he knows what must have been.

How it was they found the upper room where the tableboard was set, where the supper meal was laid. How a woman and her sister made the meal that they would eat. How they pounded millet seed and amaranth for a day. How they dipped the dates in honey. Soaked the lentils. Milked the goat.

How the woman knew to carry them the bread she baked unleavened. How she carried her bucket to the well, and fetched the water, held the ladle to the bowl but did not pour. How she shaped the loaf, instead, with water of her weeping. No pinch of salt from the sea of the dead, but the brine of her weeping.

How she took it to the place, the room, where men would meet. Walking though the rabble of the streets. Turning down the stone-paved way. Carrying her basin and the lentils and the dates. The warm loaf to her breast. The knife beneath her skirt. Heard the noise of marching around a corner. Found the soldiers in her way. Saw the breastplates muscled, burnished; cock-plume panaches sprouting from the helmets. What are you hiding there? What is that you carry? How she held the loaf and offered them a piece. How she stood while they laughed and touched their lances to her skirt until they turned away and let her be. How she found the unmarked door and climbed the unlit stair. Found the room where she knew to lay the table. Knew to set the places, bring the vessels, place the knife.

How the woman knew to bring a basin for their feet. How she brought soft cloth and soap scented with lavender. How she held the cloth in her teeth to tear it in pieces. Pulled the threads where it was frayed. Folded twelve even pieces where each one of them would sit. Where each would dry his feet. Placed the sponge. Poured the wine. Sliced the loaf. How she wiped the knife clean with her skirt and kissed the blade.

Did she leave the stone lamp unlighted? The wick twisted? The basin beneath the table? Did she know that He would want it? Did she know where He would sit?

I do not ask the bishop how they let Him wash their feet, how they watched Him kneel and crawl beneath the tableboard while they knew that soon His hands would be split to the bone and bleeding.

I do not ask what they said when they felt the sponge, the wet.

When He offered up his body, why would they want to eat?

When He said that the wine is blood, why would they take a drink?

Did the one who would betray Him keep the knife that sliced the bread?

When they offered him the silver to betray Him, did he weep?

Did he toss the coins away? Did he give them to a peddler?

Did he leave them in his pocket? Did he find the poor fishermen whose sons had walked away, left their fishing nets and fathers salt-stiff and unmended? Did he place them in the fish-scaled hands of the fathers of the fishermen, scarred by slips of the belly-gutting blades?

Did the one who betrayed Him take the knife from the table?

Was the knife that cut the bread the one he tilted to his throat?

Did the woman who was waiting keep watch in the alleyway? Did she sleep where she stood with her head against the stones?

Did the woman who was waiting find the room dark and empty? Find the stone lamp on the table, light the end of the wick, tip the pitcher to the flame? Did she see that the wine had been taken, save the dregs in her vessel? Did she see the crumbs, the crusts, the bits of bread left on the tableboard, and sweep them up into her hand, knowing she must take them?

The bishop takes the knife and cuts bread the kitchen sisters baked.

We tear apart the pieces.

The bishop wipes the smear of berries from his cheek. He brushes bits of leaf off from his shirt.

I coil my hair around my hand, twist it at my neck, and catch it with a twig. I tuck it up beneath my veil. I tie the cincture to the side above my hips.

I take the shawl up by the fringe, and shake the crumbs away. The chaffinch flutters down to eat. I tie and knot the ends of it across my breast.

We walk upon the broken ferns. We find the bitter cress along the bank and where the stream is swift. We take the leaves into our mouths. We taste the bottom mud, the grit. We taste the earth that one day we will taste. We dip the last crust into the brook.

Sister Sigrid says a blood-red moon shines through her cell window, coloring the walls, lighting the ceiling, changing the spider that hangs on its strand to a drop from the wound when His flesh was cut.

Sister Salvinia says the relic finger of Saint Agnes has become more bent and beckoning.

Sister Marjorie brings me the corn, strips off the silk gone as black as hag's hair, and shows me the kernels filled with ash and dust.

Sister Marjorie says the hedgehog has moved out of the cabbages and taken up residence amid the asparagus.

Sister Issobel says the two-headed hop that lives in the apple bin spreads its sticky toes and takes hold of her habit.

Sister Cleopas says the cock crows at all hours because his comb flops over and he cannot see if dawn has come or the sun has set.

Sister Salvinia says the billy goat has lips like the sheriff's and hairs on his chin just as prickly as the vicar's.

Sister Amanda finds Issobel and Bette kissing in the scullery when they should be scrubbing.

Issobel says when she cracked a hen's egg into the griddle grease, a black imp sprang forth and danced on the pan. It slid through the lard fat and now hides in the kitchen.

"Spill the flour bins, empty the cupboards," says the vicar. "Do what you must, but roust the demon out."

The vicar is in the priory office, tapping his foot, taking me to task.

He asks me if I know the whereabouts of the bishop. He asks if am aware there is a peddler dozing in the pig trough. Did I know that the farrow hog and her hoglets are loose in the garden, rooting through the cucumbers? Helping themselves to the asparagus, nose to nose with a hedgehog?

Did I know that Sister Salvinia is not about her duties, fetching home delinquent pigs, as she needs to be doing, but instead snoring quite loudly and tucked into the pig trough beside the peddler?

Am I aware, the vicar asks, that there are fern stalks sticking to my habit? That there are twigs caught in my hair and that my lips are quite crimson? Did I realize that my habit is unfastened? And why is it that my wimple is askew?

I do not tell the vicar how my habit comes to be unfastened.

How my hair spilled down upon the bishop's chest and belly.

I do not say that the ferns were broken with our bodies.

Am I aware, the vicar asks, that Sister Decimina takes the host on her tongue in such a way as to not wet it? Or that once she is outside and in the piggery, she feeds it in secret to the blue-spotted shoat?

"Holy Father," says the bishop, "still the trembling of our hearts."

The vicar says that the buns that Sister Amanda and the kitchen sisters bake are not plumped with sour cherries, but stuffed with clots that spill from Sister Sigrid—her feet, her hands.

"Holy Father," says the bishop. "Open up the gates of Heaven."

The vicar says that Sister Salvinia pays a daily visit to the devil, riding to hell on the billy goat's horn.

"Holy Spirit," prays the bishop, "grant us absolution; forgive us all our faltering faith."

Sister Decimina fears the one dark lamb hasn't wool enough for shearing.

Sister Heart says most shrouds are black, but not necessarily.

Sister Meg says the bee-veil gauze will keep the gravesoil off our faces.

Sister Marjorie says she will hold our mouths closed with a length of bindweed, twice around the mandible, knot-tied at the temple.

Sister Issobel thinks someone has been drinking up the cuttlefish ink.

In the garden, the cornstalks are withered. On the cob, the kernels crack and split.

Stalls are empty in the market. In the village, doors are shut.

"Discretion," says the reeve. "Bar all travelers, turn out all rovers."

"Precautions," says the sheriff. "Exclude foreigners, sailors, and anyone fevered."

"Use vigilance," says the notice, posted by the councilman:

No higglers. No pimpers. No hucksters. No tumblers.
No mummers. No jugglers. No tagalong doxies or pay-penny wenches.
No persons with tambourines, reed pipes, or timbrels.
No harp singers, sweet-sellers, minstrels, or lute players.
No cozeners, shifters, or dusty-footed beggars.

No flea-pickers, dung-vendors, privy-ditch keepers.
No loitering lepers lacking bell or clapper.
Remind those infected to stand to the leeward.
Please send away anyone crimson-faced or blistered.
Turn out anyone kerneled or sweating.
No access for anyone fevered or thinner.
No husbands of wives who have recently expired.
No wives of husbands not bringing in the harvest.
No bawds, no scamps. No scolds, no strumpets.
No slatterns, no cutpurses; no flute-toting troubadours.

"Prudence," says the bailiff. "Barricade the village gate so no one may enter. Fortify the thoroughfare; build a bonfire. It will purify the air and neutralize the vapors. Serve as a warning to vagrants and troublemakers."

"Forethought," says the vicar. "Organize a procession; outfit the cotters; a barefoot penance with goat-whips and crosses."

"Foresight," says the sheriff, nailing up the ordinance:

Address no strangers on byways or roadsides.
Make no trade with peddlers or with tinkers.
Beware of all purveyors of nog and uzzle-pie.
Purchase no furs or harbingers of vermin; no lettice, felt, or miniver.
Examine all pelts for evidence of hop-flea.
Flee from anyone walking erratically.
Hop like a minstrel who is piping on his mouth horn.
Walk upwind when walking past a plague pit.
Baptize any infants you should find by the wayside.
Pass by persons appearing wasted.
Tote a vial of holy water with you, if you are out walking.
Recite a short psalm if you are out walking and a procession of rats crosses the road.
Recite from the gospels if you are out walking and should recognize your neighbor out riding ahead of you, bare-boned to the wagon

boards, or pressed between strangers. Tossed in a pile or else stacked for efficiency—scapula to breast, buttock to belly—ajoggle in the horse cart of the dead.

You may see the face of the smith or the weaver. It may be the foot of a lover or rover. It may be a hand hanging over the wagonside; a ring overlooked by the dead-cart driver, by the quicklime boy and by the town pit-digger.

You may see the face of the miller or baker. It may be the face of that tavern maid you wanted. The one you thought so rosy as she leaned across the table. The one who was laughing, who rebuked your advances. The one so buxom. The one so merry.

Can you hear her now above the creak of the dead-cart? Now her hair is let down, pale and powdered by the road dust, or tangled in the wheel spoke. She smiles for you now, with her jaw stiff shut, lips pulled above the teeth and tongue lolled against a stranger's warty loins or scabby feet.

She would not rebuff you now, if you still would like to have her. If you still think that you want her. She would offer no resistance.

Except, perhaps, a stiffness in her haunches. A chill of the cleft. But she might still be soft if the worms have begun.

Be sure to examine her hairy parts for vermin.

Be sure to wash your privy-limb with quicklime and seawater. Use a soft cloth, preferably scented with lavender.

Then rinse yourself well with lime juice and rose water.

Fold the cloth when you are finished, and toss into a street fire. (We will keep many burning for your convenience.)

Fold her hands across her breast before the driver lifts the pin and the wagon hatch is opened; the floor board tilts; she slides into the pit; quick-lime is shoveled over.

Indulge in these simple pleasures with what time may still be left to you: soon enough it will be a serpent that comes sucking at your privy limb.

Undersigned: the vicar; sanctioned by the bailiff; the steward in full agreement.

This day, the ninth of February, this year of our Lord, thirteen hundred forty-nine.

The peddler is at the priory gate, plying his trade, exhibiting his inventory. The peddler has the lime juice. The peddler has the rose water. And should the vicar have the need to post another notice, the peddler has the inkpots, quill pens, parchment. Nails for tacking up emergency bulletins. Hammers for hammering. In fact, he has the very hammer. And with it, of course, the original nail—the one left over, saved by a centurion with enterprise and aforethought who decided to use only three.

The peddler has paper freshly pressed from far Manchuria. Official wax and official seals should the sheriff have the need for posting something more to say.

The peddler has the relics. He has what will preserve us: parts of a saint from the rape of Constantinople, long concealed in a tub of brine-cured pork.

The peddler has the originals; he has what we are needing: pieces of the apostles, prized by collectors, and everyday objects touched by their holy hands: Saint Matthew's fishing net; Saint Jude's compass; Saint Luke's mortar; Saint Mark's pestle.

The pot the Holy Infant is known to have pissed in, certified and dated.

The peddler has what no other peddler peddles: Saint Simon's molar. Saint Andrew's incisor. The tooth of the whale that swallowed Jonah.

The peddler has items once thought lost to the ages: John the Baptist's breechcloth. Salome's platter. Extra olives from the press at Gethsemane. Assorted spare doubts from St. Thomas.

The peddler has what Christ himself would have wanted to hide in His pocket, if only He could find it.

What might have saved Our Savior if He'd only met a peddler; what can save you now if you invest in protection: treasures of the ancients long thought to be lost and just recently rediscovered; mementos of the Moses plague—a locust trapped in amber; a flask of blood when the Nile was drained of water. A chip of the tablets.

Ask without hesitation, if you don't see what you're looking for: an ember from the burning bush in perpetual conflagration? Goat dung imprinted with a footprint of Noah? The stone that felled Goliath?

The peddler has the relics worthy of your veneration: the core of the apple. A hinge from the garden gate of Eden (rusted, but serviceable).

("Bogus," says the sheriff, of tidings from the southland: so many serfs have perished that knights must plow their fields themselves, and churchmen must thresh the corn.)

The peddler has the Word on a scrap of ancient parchment— the Word that was with God in the beginning.

Calligraphies in ink from Dead Sea cuttlefish sealed in beeswax.

And lastly, the peddler has an item that is most remarkable; what may look to the untrained observer to be the skin of some leviathan or the flakes of a creature submersible and marine; what appears to be ordinary fish scales sealed in a bottle is actually something put aside when the firmament was dark. Is actually a left-over illumination once held in the hand of the Creator, scattered across the water to bring on the dawn and to let there be light.

A bit of scintillation, some surplus flash and splendor—beams that would be helpful if the apocalypse comes early.

The peddler has what will save us, protect and spare us.

("Sham," says the vicar, of news from Dorset abbey: serpents in a chalice, worms in the pyx.)

"Such purchases," says the vicar, "will hardly be necessary; your information is quite faulty; there is no forthcoming calamity."

"I am, however," says the vicar, "impressed with your selection. Do come round next season and show us something more."

The vicar tells the bishop we must plan for future purchases; we must examine the treasury, consider new attractions; we must alow for our share of a profit in the pilgrimages.

The vicar tells the bishop that he has spied him in the forest, naked and knee-down like a feral pig rooting truffles; that he has seen my bishop on all-fours in the woodland greenery with the horse-bit in his mouth and me astride his back.

The bishop brings a letter from the abbot of Dorset. It is tattered but readable and here in its entirety:

Bishop, old friend:

My salutations to you with this missal, but I fear it may be my last. There is no cause for concern, however, as all is well here at the abbey—but due to ensuing circumstances, I can no longer secure reliable couriers. We are all hale and well, but I can find no traveler who will guarantee delivery. We have been plagued by a shortage of goose quills. I am nearly out of paper. No pestilence has appeared in these regions—for that, praise be to God—but I am almost out of ink.

Have your heard, dear bishop, that each new moon brings a peak in the mortality?

I have suffered lately from headaches and confusion.

Is it true the vicar's palfrey was devoured by the cottars?

And by the way, old friend, may I ask a favor of you? If Sister Marjorie is still planting her garden, would it be at all possible for her to send some seeds of lavender? We have vestments here to be scented; there are sheets that are fouled in need of freshening; there is the occasional coffin that would benefit from a floral decoration; there are graves—however shallow—that could use a pretty planting. I remember waking in the priory to the lovely smell of lavender. Does Sister Decimina still smell of goat rut? I remember finding a sprig of lavender beneath the pillow. I remember sniffing the delightful fragrance on the sheets spread beneath me.

I recall the dungish smell of Sister Decimina on the sheets spread beneath me.

May I ask, at this late date, if you have ever been tempted? Have you seen the farrow hog, the favorite of Decimina's, with a row of piglets on its nipples, and perhaps thought to suck upon on the teats of the prioress?

May I ask, since time is limited, if you have ever so been tempted?

May I inquire, since these times are quite uncertain, if you have ever been so tempted?

May I ask if you have gazed upon the painting of the Holy Mother? The one that hangs on the wall in the priory? I noticed it there when last I visited. I am sure you know the one of which I am speaking—the gilt-framed oil near the window in the nave. I refer to that loving posture so wonderfully captured: her garments laid open, her pale bosom offered to the Holy Infant seated in her lap. Have you perceived that His smile seems to be of unholy anticipation?

Did I mention that I frequently have periods of dizziness and confusion?

We have had less sunny days than one would anticipate, for such a dry summer.

Despite all reports to the contrary, the wheat yield appears substantial; unfortunately, however, we lack countrymen to bring in the harvest.

It is wise, they say, to put aside the grain that will be usable. An amount thought to be reasonable. Though it is likely, they say, that there will be no one left to devour it. It is probable, they say, that no one will be spared the pestilence, that the world will not recover. It will be as in the beginning, when the garden was unblemished. Before the light made us visible. Before the land was made. Before the seas were full of fishes, and the firmament dark. Before the word was with us, and the first word was spoken.

Blessings hereby sent to those with you who may be surviving.

In the name of the one we now know to be unholy and unrisen

and who gives no thought to save us,
   Alfred, Abbot of Dorset,
   On this, the twentieth of February, thirteen hundred forty-nine.

In the field, the wheat is ready. The skep, we hope, is full of honey. There is hawkweed at the roadside, feverfew in the garden, columbine nodding where the pig trough leaks. The bees light, the stems sway. The petals bend as their tongues find the nectar and they lift away with blossom dust clinging to their feet.

In the scullery, we wash the jars we will use to save the honey. We melt the wax to seal the lids. We sharpen the blade to slice through the comb. We plait the stalks of gorse, fray the ends, and hang them on fire from the hook and beam. We pray that the smoke will put the bees to sleep.

Sister Meg says that honeybees all beat their wings too fast for us to see them.

The bishop says that it must be the same with saints and angels, and so it is for Sister Sigrid when we wonder by what means she lifts herself to the ceiling of her cell; that she must bear a set of wings we never see but needs for flight.

"Not wings alone," says our anchoress Sister Sigrid from behind her curtained window. "Not wings, nor faith alone, but earth," says Sister. "The earth the bee takes in her feet to give her weight, to keep the world beside her in her flight, to know the earth unto her death."

Sunday comes; the mass is said. Reeve and miller, bailiff, wife and cotter are in the aisle and before the rail. Baker, peddler, clerk of the manor; the sheriff who has never come, on his knees, head down to the bishop. Mason and steward, midwife and serf say their prayers, place their trust. Laborer, smith, field lad, ferryman, bent-legged beggar all close their eyes, hope and swallow. We hear the psalm. The bishop leads the singing.

The vicar speaks of rumor; the bishop preaches retribution. The censer smokes. The beeswax candles sputter.

The bishop bends to kiss the miller's children. All but one is in attendance—the youngest feeling unwell, just this morning.

Sister Salvinia opens the reliquary. We view the martyr's blood that clots the sand. We see the shriveled finger. We pass and touch our foreheads. We kneel and hear the bishop speak the holy words before the host. He holds it in his hands above us: pale moon, holy food—mild and unbroken, unrent and bloodless. He lifts it above us, as ascended as the body.

We take the bread again, for our evening meal together. The bishop breaks the loaf. Sister Amanda says the grace. The kitchen sisters set the platters on the trestle table. We pass the stew of leek; we lift the crock of curded cheese; we pass the mead, the autumn apples, the honey cake.

All are quiet, waiting for the reading. "Lectio divinia." I open the book:

And the Lord bade Moses, "Go with the children of Israel; make a feast in the wilderness, and a sacrifice to serve me." But the pharaoh's heart was hardened and he would not let them go.

"Like an old broody hen when you reach for her egg," says Sister Cleopas, pouring the mead.

And the Lord bade Moses, "Take up handfuls of ashes of the furnace, and fling them towards heaven in the sight of the pharaoh and before those whose hearts are hardened, and let them be carried on the wind."

"Like the chaff in the dove dish when the millet seeds are gone," says Sister Heart, spearing the leek.

And the ash shall be blown as a dust in all the land, and become a boil breaking forth with blains upon man, and galls upon beast.

"Like a tick getting fat in the billy goat's beard," says Sister Salvinia, cracking a beechnut in her teeth.

And I will send plagues such as these upon the people, and all whose hearts are hardened will believe.

I do not ask the bishop how it is that he believes.

I do not wake him while he lies beside me in the wood.

He does not feel my hand along his cheek. Not my kisses on his neck. Not my palm along his loins.

He does not know that now I kneel inside this glade. That I clasp my hands and look to Heaven, to the limbs above our heads gone nearly bare of leaves, to the sky beyond the branches: the evening clouds, the fading of the day. That there comes no light from Heaven; no pinions of the angels; no blessed shed of feathers. Just the drift and fall of leaves.

He does not know that there is no sign from Heaven. That I watch him as he sleeps with his head upon the moss.

He does not feel my fingers move along his hip to the hollow of his groin. The place I find the gall, the early blister; the hard mound of his flesh.

In the garden, the gourds are hollow. Seeds rattle.

In the kitchen, Sister Amanda pits the sour cherries. Sister Issobel pours the sugar. Sister Bette stirs the jam.

At the rope tied tree-to-tree for laundry, Sister Helen and Sister Johanna face each other. The sheet between them, their hands at each corner. Meeting each other; now hands together, making the fold, smoothing the cloth.

In the infirmary, the beds are ready. Clean ticking. Fresh pillows. The medicinals are bottled, aligned and labeled: aconite, belladonna, coltsfoot, dogbane; ergot, foxglove, flower of hemlock; syrup of ipecac, jimson, kenilworth; tea of live-forever, mandrake, nightshade; opium, pepperwort, quinine leaf; dried rose-mallow, self-heal, touch-me-not; vetchweed, wormwood, yarrow-grass flower.

In the infirmary, the blood-basin is waiting. The blade is sharp. The letting cords ready. The leeches sleep in their boggy pot. The soap is scented, caked, and cured. On the shelf, the shrouds are stacked.

In the dovecote, Sister Pigeon is whispering, advising her birds of the best route to the sea.

In the kitchen, the board is floured. Our hands are white, our skirts our dusted. The dough is rising. The pans are greased.

In the yard, Sister Cleopas hoists the grain sack. The ruff-legged hens levitate from their dust-bath hollows. Sister Cleopas spills the feed and fills the trough. The brood of chicks all lift up and come.

In the garden, Sister Meg is in her bee-veil. The skep is heavy. The queen is missing: buzz and hover. The comb is full.

In the hopfield, at the edge of forest, Sister Pigeon wets her finger. She feels the sea wind. She opens her basket: a drift of feathers. She lifts out a dove.

In the anchorage, Sister Sigrid is digging. Her mat is straw. There is earth beneath. The stones are wet. Her hands are muddied. Grit on her knees. Worms in her fingers. Nails are broken; palms bloodied. She piles the stones along her door.

In the garden, Sister Amanda is digging with her foot to the shovel. The sod is broken. Scraggles of stem. The dry leaves crumble. The roots severed. Stone scored by metal. The ditch is narrow. She scoops the soil over: scuttle of the millipede, cold of the pebble. Tumblebug, dung beetle. Foot, leg, breast: her body covered. Heaped at the neck. Chin to the mound. Smoothed with her fingers. Leaves fly past and cling to the gate.

On the road, the peddler is hurrying. Past the hop field. Past the hawkweed. Strap and twine, sack and bundle. The hurdy-gurdy crank is still now. Hollow clink of pan and crockery. The wheel-spokes turn. The cart boards creak.

In the kitchen, Sister Amanda pokes her finger in the squares of the sweet dough. Sister Bette spoons the jam inside. Sister Issobel pinches it over.

On the table, a dish is red with the stones of cherries.

The oven is hot. The rack is set. The pan of rolls is lifted in.

Blood moon cresting the south-slope rise.

The dough swells. The jam leaks.

The gauze is folded. The gorse is ready. We follow Sister Meg into the garden. We hear the buzzing in the skep. Sister Heart says the gauze is blessed with the prayer of her spinning. Sister Meg says it will keep the bees from our faces. Sister Helen has the stalks of gorse to light and set to smoldering. Sister Amanda totes along the embers in her scuttle. Sister Marjorie carries the tin of grease. Sister Bette has the knife to cut the hive and honeycomb. Sister Cleopas has the basket to hold the pieces. Sister Pigeon brings the bindweed for wrapping our hands. Sister Johanna has the tin of balm to soothe the welts if our prayers have been unheard, if our hearts have been soiled, if our faith wings away.

We drape the lengths of gauze along our shoulders. We tie the ends across our breasts. The wind begins to rise with the twilight coming, the night air cooling. It lifts the cloth from off my back. The edges rise, the folds billow. Swell in the gusts. Whip at the tatters. If I loosened the knot, it would fly from my fingers.

If I stood at the wood edge and held on tight, would the wind lift me up? Sail me away? It would carry me above the wood, over the priory; past the dovecote and the piggery. Over the town and the south country hop-fields. Above chancellery and steeple, where the tolling bells are swinging; over the treetops where the carrion crows are waiting.

It would take me through the coming dusk, above the pits and the lantern flames of the pit-diggers, high above the bonefires and the barns left burning. Over the boats of the fishermen, ignited and abandoned; over the crosses made out of mast and spar with their crows' nests in flames and the bowsprits blazing. Over beach and dune to the driftwood pyres, to the camps of the dying and the fires of men driven to the edge of the sea.

I will carry there the bottle of fish-scale and shimmer strapped fast to my foot with the jess of leather.

I will watch the lights in the towns go out. See the village wife sweep the last mouse and last rat from the step. See the edge of the village grave where the townsfolk stand, sway and faint, close in, step to the brink—the ragged fringe of turf and root, the crumbling clods of soil that break the foothold and let them slip. Let them drop upon each other, while the last digger waits and the height for falling to the bottom grows less.

I will see the last digger lean himself against his shovel, give the ones too tired to jump their final elbow in. Give the ones who need a moment's pause a needed push. Tap the shoulder of the one who wants to say her prayers, but braces herself for the final shove.

High above him, I will watch the last digger. He will stand at the brink and toss his lantern in. He will watch the bright arc of the wick light the faces. He will hear the glass break when the light finds the bottom. He will clamber down and follow in the stinking dark. And I will drift far above him on the smoke of the bonefire, aloft on the breath of the dead.

And when the last ember is ash, and the firmament goes dark again above the shifting waters, could I wing over the beach, lift above the bay? Breaking the bottle seal, and loosening the cork. Strewing the scales, the light left over, wet with the spray of the high-riding sea.

In the company of doves, on the wind-wake of the flock. Ahead of the peregrine. Outwinging the harrier. Tatter-winged and Heavenbound, evading the kestrel hawk.

Uplifted and believing, without a place to light.

Sister Meg lifts the gauze from off our shoulders. She gathers it in folds upon our heads, wraps our hands and ties the bindweed at the cuffs. We take the twisted wands of gorse and dip the frayed ends in the grease. We touch them to the embers for a flame and wave them out.

We clutch the stalks and draw the glowing ends across the air, making our letters with the bright calligraphy of fire. We move the tapers, form the words. Our scepters flare. We trace our final inscriptions with the tendrils of the light.

We make our ciphers in the dark until the incandescence dims. Until the straws go out. They twist themselves apart. We send away the last epistles of the heat.

We lift the folds of gauze we wear and let the gathers fall. The drape of it before our eyes is thin enough for seeing.

We hold our wands of ash. We have our withered filaments of dust.

The hive is full of singing.

We face the smoke.

With gratitude to George Rand, David McLendon, Peter Markus, and to the staff at Dzanc: Daniel Wickett, Steve Gillis, Matt Bell, Steven Seighman.